Robert B. Vance

Heart-Throbs from the Mountains

Robert B. Vance

Heart-Throbs from the Mountains

ISBN/EAN: 9783337289515

Printed in Europe, USA, Canada, Australia, Japan

Cover: Foto ©Andreas Hilbeck / pixelio.de

More available books at **www.hansebooks.com**

Heart - Throbs

From The Mountains.

By Robert

*My soul is full of other .... outh returns.
Thus the sun appears in th............ of his brightness have moved behind .... ills lift their
dewy heads ; the blue stre............* —OSSIAN.

Sout............SE.

DEDICATION.

TO THE

GOOD PEOPLE

OF THE

Dear Old Eighth Congressional District

OF NORTH CAROLINA,

Who for so many years have given
their support and friendship to the writer, in the public
affairs of the country as well as
in the sweet and joyful
relations of private life,

THE FOLLOWING PAGES

ARE

AFFECTIONATELY DEDICATED

BY THE AUTHOR.

To the Reader.

~~~~~~

THE writer does not pretend that these effusions are brilliant or beautiful. They are the outgrowth of feeling, and were written, for the most part, from time to time, as circumstances suggested them, without any fixed purpose to present them in book form. The author is anxious, and fully purposes (D. V.), to build a church at Riverside, N. C., his place of residence; and the profits, if any, arising from the sale of the book will go to that object.

The prison pieces were written at Fort Delaware in 1864–5, which will account for some show of feeling in the great struggle then raging.

With the earnest hope that these verses may be beneficial to his readers, the author commits his little book to their kind consideration.

R. B. V.

Washington City, January 14, 1887.

Contents.

8   *Contents.*

Heart-Throbs from the Mountains.

THE OLD NORTH STATE.

HAIL, good old mother, dear and beautiful
  In our glad eyes, we worship at thy feet
With all the ardor of fond, dutiful
   Children, who with a true affection greet
   The one whose love has made their lives so sweet!

Precious old State! Each pulse that thrills
  In rushing tide from the full heart,
Free as her own swift mountain rills,
  Shall hold for thee a faithful part,
While the sun's first streak kisses ocean's cheek
And wraps in fire each mighty mountain peak.

    Ah! yes, indeed,
    We bring our meed
To place it on thy honored, queenly brow,
  That earth may see the chivalry
  Of sons whose fathers bled for thee—
A race as true in days gone by as now.

When Freedom's banner was unfurled
In this our glorious Western World,
  The first dear gush of patriot blood
  Which for the cause of freemen flowed,
Where sword and spear gave shining glance,
Was on thy field—red Alamance!*
  And there thy sons, with dirk and glave,

---

* The battle of Alamance was fought in May, 1771.

(2)   (9)

Stood forth, a rank as stern and brave
As e'er a field of battle trod,
And gave their lives for thee and God.

And further too, it was to thee
And thy staunch sons that Liberty
    First gained a foothold in the West; *
    Where, round the fiery "Hornet's Nest," †
The world was called to stand and view
The words of men as bold and true
As e'er a trenchant claymore drew;
    Who, looking at the Lion's paws,
    Defied his might, denounced his laws;
And there, with stern integrity,
Proclaimed this land should ever be
Independent, sovereign, free;
    Pledged fortune, life, and honor bright,
    To stand as one for each dear right,
    Or perish on the field of fight;
And each honored name is still all aflame
In thy people's hearts, who after them came.

        And on thy soil, ‡
        With bloody toil,
The chieftains of the mountain range
Made the patriot cause to change,
    When not a banner was there seen
    To wave in all that forest green;
When not a drum was heard to beat
To sound the charge, or for retreat;
    When not a bugle broke the air

---

* The western part of North Carolina.
† Charlotte Declaration of Independence, May 20, 1775.
‡ King's Mountain. The battle was fought October 7, 1780, and the field proper was on the South Carolina side of the line.

To warn the Britons posted there;
And not an ambulance had they
To bear the wounded from the fray;
  And not a surgeon with his knife
  To amputate in cause of life;
When old Virginia, and the twins,*
With stalwart men whose fighting wins,
  With deadly rifles, long and bright,
  Drove the invaders from the height;
While high upon the mountain top
They nearly caused the war to stop;
  And there each noble name, in living flame,
  They writ upon the fadeless rolls of fame.

On every field that ran with blood,
  From Lundy's Lane to Mexico,
Thy sons have by the shoulders stood,
  And answered well each deadly blow;
For coming from the Scot and Celt,
Races that always wore the belt,
  With sprinklings of the Huguenot,
  Their 'scutcheon never had a blot;
And crowning all, like stoutest granite wall,
The Anglo-Saxon, free from Norman thrall.
    But the heart stands still
    With an anguished thrill,

---

* North and South Carolina. Some accounts state that there were present, also, men from Georgia, Tennessee, and Kentucky. This is probably the force: Burke and McDowell, N. C., Colonel Charles McDowell, 160 men; Wilkes and Surrey, N. C., Colonel Benjamin Cleaveland and Major Joseph Winston, 350 men; Washington County, N. C. (now Tenn.), Colonel John Sevier 240 men; Sullivan County, N. C. (now Tenn.), Colonel Isaac Shelby, 240 men; Washington County, Va., Colonel William Campbell, 400 men; troops under Colonel George Williams, South Carolina, number not given.

When once again with banners gay,
All harnessed for the dreadful fray,
Thy children passed who wore the Gray;
  Who in a cause they deem'd the right
  Showed how the Southrons still could fight.
And from Potomac's flowing tide
To Texan prairies, fair and wide,
  On many a field, by many a stream,
  They're sleeping now their dreamless dream;
And many a home is lone and sad
Which once was by their presence glad;
  And many a lorn and humble grave,
O'er which the lilies gently wave,
  Shall tell where peaceful sleep the brave
Who died their Sunny South to save.
  And when our maidens, sweet and fair,
With love which has its tender sway,
  Shall come to strew bright flowers there,
They'll speak of those who wore the Gray;
  And they'll drop a tear o'er the lonely bier
  Where the soldier rests with his broken spear.

    But not alone
    Will sleep our own;
For side by side where they fought and died,
The Blue and Gray—our country's pride—
  Shall rest in peace till Judgment-day
  Shall call them from their beds of clay.
And there with millions yet unborn,
Upon the resurrection morn,
  Their colors will so joyful blend—
  Where one begins the other'll end—
That when we turn our dead to view,
We'll surely think that all is Blue;

But turning then the other way,
We'll feel convinced that all is Gray;
    And if the brave dead
    From each dusty bed
Shall in the joys of peace be ever wed,
    What reason can be
    'Neath Liberty's Tree
For bitterest hate in this Land of the Free?

Yes, we love thee, dear native land,
From mountain peak to ocean strand;
    Thy giant crags, thy silver streams,
    Which catch the morning's early beams;
Thy rock-bound capes, thy ocean spray,
Where the blue Gulf Stream waters play;
    Thy mighty oaks and nodding pines,
    Thy luscious fruits and teeming vines;
Thy worthy sons and daughters true,
Those strong as oak, these light as dew;
    Thy storied name among the first
    On the Atlantic shore to burst;
      Till our hearts are thine
      In love so divine
That death alone can its strong chords untwine.

HICKORY-NUT FALLS, N. C.

[The scenery of Western North Carolina is unsurpassed in the world. The gifted pen of our fair countrywoman, Christian Reid, has made portions of it famous in such works as "The Land of the Sky," "A Summer Idyl," and other stories. The Hickory-Nut Falls are situated in Rutherford County, on the eastern slope of the Blue Ridge. The water rushes over the rock and mountain at least a thousand feet above the cañon below, and over five thousand feet above tide-water. To the eye of the traveler on the highway on the north side of Broad River, the creek—large enough

beyond the Falls to turn the wheels of a mill—looks, especially
in summer, like a lady's veil, as it dashes down the sides of the
immense boulder.]

THOU rock that in thy grand and noble height
Look'st eternal!   A thousand ages gone
Thy dreadful front was lifted up in wrath
By fires volcanic in earth's young bosom.
How dost thou smile on man and mock his pride,
And teach him day by day his littleness,
When once compared to thee in majesty !
Only God, the great, omnipotent One,
Was able to rear thy fearful presence,
And by his agencies, to us unseen,
To cause thy Titan head to kiss the clouds,
And fill the beholder with solemn awe—
Once seen, to be forgotten nevermore.

The march of time, feeling for eternity;
The hurricane's sweep, encircling the hills;
The earthquake, in its direful, heaving throes,
To thee are nothing; thou art planted deep
In strength and pillared stability by Him —
The God, and Maker, and Monarch of all.

And you, ye murmuring, glittering waters,
Which leap in beauty o'er this giant cliff,
Your soothing tones have charmed these silent dells
With silvery music since creation's morn,
Arrayed in rosy light, was ushered in,
E'en when the morning stars together sang,
And all the sons of God shouted for joy.
Beyond the rock thy silver founts are hid
Where oft in nature's freedom, sweet and glad,
The Indian maid hath loosed her raven hair,

And, joyful gazing at the form there seen,
Has decked it gay with fragrant flowers wild.

And you, ye stately, tall, and shadowing pines
Which stand unbent, unmoved by elemental strife:
O'er your tops, which tower erect, and proudly nod
To heaven's e'erlasting arch, the eagle screams,
And, bending from his flight beneath the sun,
Upon your boughs his lofty eyrie builds.

And you, ye mountains high on either hand,
Which rear in grandeur dread each hoary crest,
And, peering through clouds that hover nigh,
Present a monument of power sublime
Connected fast with wisdom's wondrous might—
From your high peaks the thunder's lifted voice
Has ofttimes shook the globe on which we live,
And there the lightning's fierce and vivid flash
In sportive freak with bright and fiery wing
Has wrapped in flame each bare and rugged scalp.

And oft in days that long have passed away,
Upon those cliffs that shoot out o'er the vale,
The chieftain's eye, all fired with manly pride,
Has scanned his hunting-ground; and as the buck,
With many a bound secure, went swiftly by,
The arrow left the warrior's high-strung bow,
And, quivering in the stag's bold heart, gave proof
Of the red man's deadly aim and fatal skill.

But nevermore, by peak, or fall, or plain,
Shall his wild whoop disturb these scenes again.
The pale face came—the red man left his home,
With saddened heart the prairied world to roam;
And maiden fair, and victor crowned with glory,
Will pause and sigh—so mournful is his story.

A DREAM.

[Written on receiving the photograph of Miss E. D. P., of Louis-
ville, Kentucky.]

THE bay was calm, the sky serene,
    The sunlight on the island,*
And Spring had tinged with robe of green
    The valley and the highland;
Sweet flowers, too, were peeping up
    Where Winter'd reigned so hoary,
And Nature held her flowing cup,
    Rejoicing in her glory.

Yet true it was, though sore to tell,
    Amid this scene of gladness
Full many a hero's heart did swell
    With much of manly sadness;
For while the waves did lave the strand
    In freedom never broken,
The prison'd one from fair Southland
    Was war's most gloomy token.

The day wore on, and by and by
    The moon shone forth in splendor,
While thousand stars bedeck'd the sky,
    Their tribute God to render;
And on this plain so wondrous bright
    The weary eye was gleaming,
Till host and gem passed from his sight—
    The captive then was dreaming.

Beside him there fair Ellen stood
    In all her maiden beauty,
And with soft voice but glowing mood

---

* Fort Delaware is on an island.

Proclaimed the brave man's duty:
"Go, soldier, go! On yon red field
The 'stars and bars' are flying;
Nor aught on earth shall make thee yield
Where freedom's sons are dying!"

With joyful breast and flashing eye
The captive knelt before her;
But, O! alas! not she was nigh,
That he might there adore her!
Each waking sense spoke forth the truth,
Though sure it made him sadder;
It was no form of joy and youth,
But only the bright shadow.

Fort Delaware, 1864.

THE SOUTH.

My Sunny South! my Sunny South!
Thou land of joy to me;
The blissful clime where sinless youth
Was spent in peaceful glee;
To-night from bars and prison walls,
On pinions light and free,
My spirit breaks its many thralls
And wildly seeks for thee!

O'er hill and brake and rushing tide,
And city's lofty spire,
And silver stream and valley wide—
The home of son and sire—
With tireless wing and swelling heart,
Which nought around may stay,
I'll burst these chords and chains apart
And seek thee far away!

The eye may droop, the form may bend,
  The hair be touched with gray;
Nor night nor morn bless'd peace may send
  To cheer the captive's way;
But sentry's tread, nor musket bright,
  Nor all the dread array
Which Northmen use to show their might,
  Can cause the soul to stay!

I'll seek thy fields and woodlands wild,
  Thy own savannahs fair,
And be again the happy child
  That liv'd and sported there;
And when in sleep I view thy streams,
  Which flow forever free,
My gladdest, brightest, sweetest dreams
  Shall be of home and thee!

Fort Delaware, 1864.

STANZAS TO A LADY.

[When the author was eighteen years old he had penned these
lines on the counter of the old James M. Smith store, in Asheville,
N. C., when Colonel P. W. Roberts, his beloved friend, stepped in,
saw the lines, rushed to the hotel with them, and gave them to the
lady. O!]

LADY! could charms like thine inspire
  A humble muse like mine,
Then would I grasp the sleeping lyre
  And sing at beauty's shrine;
But smiles more bright than poet's skill
  Can weave in song or rhyme,
Play o'er thy brow, and, ling'ring still,
  Grace there thy youthful prime.

The velvet petal of the rose,
  All moist with morning's dew,
Is not more soft than ever glows
  Thy cheek's own brilliant hue,
That sparkling eye breathes forth a tale
  Of love so pure and deep
That one might breast the storm-king's gale
  To that full harvest reap.

But not alone thy queen-like grace
  Claims tribute as its due ;
For mirror'd in thy lovely face
  Is goodness, sweet and true.
A heart like thine I know can feel
  That grief which others show,
And, with thy winning manner, steal
  A portion of their woe.

O may thy life be ever blest,
  Nor grief, nor cares, nor fears
Disturb thy hope of joyful rest
  Beyond this " vale of tears ! "
But, gathering strength each happy hour,
  As faith and love are giv'n,
Triumph at last o'er death's dread power,
  And live with God in heaven.

LINES

To Mrs. Col. W. P. B., Lexington, Ky., from whom the author received a bouquet while a prisoner at Camp Chase, Ohio.

EACH weary day the prisoner's languid eye
Could only catch the blue and tranquil sky,

As time, with silent tread, went passing by
  To visit earth and man no more.
The hated walls shut out the forest green,
The pleasant woodland wild, and sylvan scene;
And e'en the birds, which sing the boughs between,
  Were hidden too by lock and door.

And aching hearts were sadly beating there;
And faithful ones breathed forth the earnest prayer
For wife and babes, and suff'ring country fair—
  The patriot's hope and chiefest joy;
And one I knew whose inmost soul did bleed
For his lov'd South, in this her time of need ;
And oft his thoughts, with wildest, fondest speed,
  Would seek his love, his land, his boy.

'Twas thus he felt, when near his keeper stood
  With chilling look and aught but cheerful mood;
"A box," he said, in accents gruff and rude ;
  "Come, prisoner, come, and claim your right."
Then happy feelings shook the captive's breast;
A sweet "bouquet" was to his bosom pressed;
The lady's name with warmest words was blessed,
  Whose hand prepared the lovely sight.

O mother earth! by war thy bliss is dead!
Thy comfort's gone, thy beauty too hath fled!
And vengeance dire, and curses bitter, dread,
  Hang o'er thee like a chast'ning-rod ;
But charming woman's precious, holy love—
Thy fragrant flowers, almost like those above—
So lift us up that e'en in grief we prove
  We've something left of heav'n and God.

For her dear sake the soldier dons his brand;
For her he leads his brave, devoted band;

And words of cheer and token from her hand
   Are prized as boons which have no peer;
And should he fall by foeman's blade or spear,
With angel smile, and pity's softest tear,
She'll come with flowers to strew upon his bier,
   And kindly guard them, year by year.

AUTUMNAL MUSINGS.
(Written in 1860.)

THE solemn season of the year,
   With fitful breezes flying,
And wailing voice, is drawing near
   To see the green leaves dying.
On yon old hill I see them now,
   As one by one they're fading;
And dreary shadows pain my brow,
   So mournful is the shading.

The oak has rear'd its branches there,
   The hick'ry still will linger;
But soon each verdant robe will bear
   The touch of Autumn's finger;
The maple, too, with its green cast,
   As, standing with its fellow,
Will quickly bow it to the blast,
   And change its coat to yellow.

The birds are gone, they sing no more;
   The flowers have drooped and wither'd;
O when, O when on this dark shore
   Will they again be gather'd?

My heart feels sad as thus I gaze
  Upon each waning beauty,
And tears I'll shed o'er their last days—
  A sweet and sacred duty.

O! could I bear to look upon
  The Summer, as 'tis going,
Did not I trust, as time flies on,
  Again to see it glowing?
There is a hope my spirit owns—
  How fondly is it cherished!
They are not dead, those gentle ones—
  They surely have not perished!

Though leaf and flower have taken wing,
  The trees look bare and hoary;
The breath of God in the sweet Spring
  Will bring them back to glory!

'Tis thus I feel while viewing life,
  As on it passeth ever,
And know I'm wasting in the strife
  This side the dark, cold river.
The Autumn-time I know has come,
  The Winter soon will meet me;
The sorrows of this earthly home
  Full often now do greet me.

Yet still I'll trust my gracious Lord,
  Who ne'er a soul harasseth;
I'll to the grave,* with his dear word,
  Till by his anger passeth;
Then fondly trust, when the great day

---

* Job xiv. 13.

Shall open bright and vernal,
To leap with joy from earth's cold clay,
 And enter life eternal.

WHAT IS LIFE?

I SAW a child with beaming eye
 And shining, golden hair,
Who chased in glee a butterfly
 From stem to flowr't fair.
"'Tis life," he laughed—the sweet, wee thing—
 "To watch its happy flight,
As o'er the mead its radiant wing
 Cuts through the mellow light."

A boy stood by of noble form,
 And firm, elastic tread,
Whose dreaming look and ardor warm
 To all around him said:
"'Tis life to pass this youthful hour
 My banner wide unfurled,
And with the strength of manhood's pow'r
 Make combat with the world!"

A maiden by the altar knelt,
 The true, affianced bride
Of one for whom she deeply felt
 Love's holy, blissful tide,
And softly broke her gentle tone
 Upon my list'ning ear,
"'Tis life to know he is my own!
 Ah! mine alone fore'er!"

Forth from the crowd a hero came,
  On prancing, dashing steed,
Who oft amid the battle's flame
  Had made his foeman bleed.
"'Tis life," he cried, "to sweep the field,
  With keen and flashing blade,
Where man, and horse, and broken shield,
  In bloody heaps are laid!"

Then long I gazed on child and boy,
  The maiden in her bloom,
And scrutinized the bounding joy
  Which gilds the victor's plume;
And queried in my inmost heart,
  My soul with feeling rife,
Is this for truth our only part?
  Can this, indeed, be "life?"

As thus I stood, an aged man
  Went slowly, feebly by,
Whose hoary locks and closing span
  Proclaimed the time to die.
"'Tis life," he said, with parting breath,
  "To know our sins forgiven,
To gain the victory over death,
  That we may live in heaven."

LINES

Written in the Autographic Album of Mrs. M. L. Benham,
of Kentucky.

If heartfelt thanks and blessings warm
  For words of kindness spoken;
If true regard may prove a charm
  To be fore'er unbroken;

Then take them, with the earnest prayer
Of one thou hast befriended,
That peace and joy may be thy share
When time itself hath ended!

Fort Delaware, 1864.

CHAIN AND CROSS.

[The chain and cross accompanying this note were made by the
hands of Robert B. Vance and Lucius H. Smith, of North Carolina
prisoners of war, as a memorial of their gratitude for the kindness
shown them by Mrs. Mark Cartwright, Nashville, Tenn., to whom
they are hereby presented.]

By loving hands each link was twined;
By loving hands the cross suspended;
While fervent prayers and wishes kind
For her and hers were sweetly blended.
The chain will tell with silent tone
That sin may chain the soul within us;
The cross will speak of Mercy's throne,
And Him who came and died to win us.

Fort Delaware, 1864.

THERE'S BEAUTY EVERYWHERE.

Beautiful!
How beautiful is all this visible world!
How glorious in its action and itself!—*Byron.*

THERE'S beauty
In the baby grace of early childhood.
The laughing eye, the softly dimpled chin,
The velvet hair, like down on birdlet's wing;
The tiny hands that pull at "Papa's" beard;
The little mouth, where honey lingers long,

3

And which thrills us with its sweet "My Mamma."
'Twas such as these the loving Jesus took
Into his arms and, smiling, blest them there,
And beauty's stamp is on them each and all.

                    There's beauty
In the sturdy tread of playful boyhood.
The light and gleeful bound and joyous whoop;
The animated shout and echo deep;
The fresh young mind, with vigor radiant;
The spirit keen, aglow with sunlit hopes,
Where disappointment's blight not yet hath fell;
A hand to us unseen doth beck him on
To fields of fame and deeds of true renown,
Casting o'er him its glad and magic spell.

                    There's beauty
In the fairy step of happy girlhood.
The fragile form, so like the tender flower;
The bonny face, so lovely in its smile;
The gentle heart, so trusting in its truth.
Her very weakness—when to man compared,
So like the vine which clusters 'round the oak
And sheds its fragrance 'mong the leafy boughs—
Is passing fair, exceeding beautiful.

                    There's beauty
In manhood's walk and strong, defiant look.
'Mong the things of time there's none so noble.
The forest beast of fierce and tameless pride
Doth shun his eye and seek again its lair,
While high in heaven the keen-eyed eagle bold
Doth shriek its fear of him and fly his glance.
Yet 'mid it all—though king of earth he be—

His heart is strung to womanly goodness,
And mercy's works oft beautify his life.

There's beauty
In the chasten'd and mellow eve of age.
'Tis like the setting sun of pleasant days,
When skies are blue and clouds are glossed with gold;
Life's work perchance is o'er, and finished well,
Nor cares detain the part immortal here.
The friends of years, of manhood, and of age
Do gather 'round to catch the whisper'd word,
The last of earth, almost the first of heav'n—
And see how beauty gilds the dying saint.

There's beauty
Too—charming, grand—in Nature's peerless brow,
As the wing'd steeds of wrath are loosen'd
In elemental conflict dread and wild,
While in the void electric squadrons wheel
And measure keep with earthquake strides below.
Then, in the calm that storms do leave, the bow
Of peace doth span the circumambient air
With colors brighter far than painter's dreams,
Wrapping the soul in beauty soft and mild.

But, O! there's beauty
That's "sweeter still than this, than these, than all,"
In prophet's views, which flash on mortal ken,
Of blood-washed bands that chant their songs on high,
And banners wave upon the jasper walls
And pearly gates of Eden's wondrous home!
Nor this alone; the fields of bliss do ope
In verdant meads and never-fading flowers;
And 'bove them all, in beauty unalloyed,
The Throne of God abides forevermore!

LINES.

[We know a great deal about war now; but, dear readers, the Southern women know more. Blood has not dripped on our door-sills yet; shells have not burst above our homesteads. Let us pray they never may.—*Frank Leslie's Illustrated Newspaper.*]

MANY a gray-haired sire has died,
  As falls the oak to rise no more,
Because his son, his prop, his pride,
  Breath'd out his last all red with gore.
No more on earth, at morn, at eve,
  Shall age and youth entwine as one,
Nor father, son, for either grieve;
  Life's race, alas! for both is done!

Many a mother's heart has bled
  While gazing on her darling child,
As in its tiny eyes she read
  The father's image, kind and mild;
For ne'er again his voice will cheer
  The widowed heart which mourns him dead,
Nor will his kisses dry the tear
  Fast falling on the orphan's head!

Many a little form will stray
  Adown the glen and o'er the hill,
And watch with wistful looks the way
  For him whose step is missing still;
And when the twilight steals apace
  O'er mead and brook and lonely home,
And shadows cloud the dear, sweet face,
  The cry will be, "O, papa, come!"

Many a home's in ashes now
  Where joy was once a constant guest,
And mournful groups there are, I trow,
  Who've neither house nor place to rest;

And blood is on the broken sill,
　　Where happy feet of erst did go;
And everywhere, by field and rill,
　　Are sick'ning sights and sounds of woe.

There is a God who rules on high—
　　The widow's and the orphan's friend—
Who sees each tear and hears each sigh
　　That these lone hearts to Him may send;
And when in wrath He tears away
　　The reasons poor which men indite,
The record-book will plainer say
　　Who's in the wrong, and who is right.

Fort Delaware, 1864.

TO COUSIN BETTIE D., OF TENNESSEE.

A TOKEN only is this ring;
　　Its value is but trifling, too;
Yet, though 'tis but a tiny thing,
　　'Twill speak of friendship pure and true.
Dear Bettie, let it ever cling
　　'Round thy finger, a tribute due;
And then our hearts will constant spring
　　To bind our souls in love anew.

Fort Delaware, 1864.

DEATH IN THE BRIDAL CHAMBER.

AN INCIDENT OF THE BOMBARDMENT OF CHARLESTON.

FORT DELAWARE, DEL., May 12, 1864.

To the Editor of the *New York News:* You have doubtless seen
the "Incident in the Siege of Charleston," wherein the death of
Miss Anna Pickens is recorded. I have clipped the article from
the *Charleston Mercury* and added some verses to it. As the "lines"
contain nothing contraband, you can publish them if you choose to
do so. They are simple, but such as the heart of a North Carolina,

soldier feels for his fair and unfortunate countrywoman. Yours respectfully,   ROBT. B. VANCE, Brig.-Gen., etc., C. S. A.

AN INCIDENT IN THE BOMBARDMENT OF CHARLESTON.

[From the Charleston Mercury, April 24, 1864.]

The Yankees, from time to time, throw a shell into the city, and nobody seems to mind it. But misfortune willed that yesterday a shell should throw the entire community into mourning.

Miss Anna Pickens, the daughter of our former Governor, never consented to leave the city. Despite the representation of General Beauregard, she remained, braving shells and Greek-fire, tending the wounded and cheering all by her presence. Among the wounded officers under her care was Mr. Andrew De Rochelie, a descendant of one of the noblest Huguenot families of this city. This young man was full of the liveliest gratitude for his fair nurse; gratitude gave birth to a more tender sentiment; his suit was listened to; Governor Pickens gave his consent, and the marriage was fixed for yesterday, the 23d of April.

Lieutenant De Rochelle was on duty at Fort Sumter in the morning, and it was determined that the ceremony should take place at the residence of General Bonham in the evening at seven o'clock. At the moment when the Episcopal clergyman was asking the bride if she was ready, a shell fell upon the roof of the building, penetrated to the room where the company were assembled, burst and wounded nine persons, and among the rest, Miss Anna Pickens. We cannot describe the scene that followed. Order was at last re-established, and the wounded were removed—all except the bride, who lay motionless upon the carpet. Her betrothed, kneeling and bending over her, was weeping bitterly and trying to staunch the blood that welled from a terrible wound under her left breast. A surgeon came and declared that Miss Pickens had not longer than two hours to live. We will paint the general despair.

When the wounded girl recovered her consciousness, she asked to know her fate. They hesitated to tell her. "Andrew," she said, "I beg you to tell me the truth. If I must die, I can die worthy of you." The young soldier's tears were his answer, and Miss Anna, summoning all her strength, attempted to smile. Nothing could be more heart-rending than to see the agony of this brave girl, struggling in the embrace of death, and against a terrible mortal pain. Governor Pickens, whose courage is known, was almost without consciousness, and Mrs. Pickens looked upon her child with the dry, haggard eye of one whose reason totters.

Lieutenant De Rochelle was the first to speak. "Anna," he cried, 'I will die soon, too, but I would have you die my wife. There is yet time to unite us."

The young girl did not reply; she was too weak. A slight flush rose for an instant to her pale cheek; it could be seen that joy and pain were struggling in her spirit for the mastery. Lying on a sofa, her bridal dress all stained with blood, her hair disheveled, she had never been more beautiful. Helpless as she was, Lieutenant De Rochelle took her hand and requested Rev. Mr. Dickinson to proceed with the ceremony. When it was time for the dying girl to say Yes, her lips parted several times, but she could not articulate. At last the word was spoken, and a slight foam rested upon her lips. The dying agony was near. The minister sobbed as he proceeded with the ceremony. An hour after all was over, and the bridal chamber was the chamber of death.

Lieutenant De Rochelle has sworn to perish in battle against the Yankees, and we are sure that he will keep his oath. He has now a double motive to hate them and his own existence.

Our entire community share the grief that afflicts the family of Governor Pickens. The obsequies of Miss Anna will take place to-morrow morning at eleven o'clock. Governor Pickens and Lieutenant De Rochelle will be chief mourners. Our ex-Governor desires that there shall be no military parade. The funeral cortege will be composed of all our ladies, all our magistrates, all our generals, and the wounded soldiers, many of whom owe their lives to the devotion of the deceased. Never has a woman been followed to the grave by so many regrets—never has one left sadder remembrances in the hearts of Charlestonians.

THE snow-white robe was placed upon
   The maiden's lithe and graceful form,
And near her stood the gallant one
   Who won her in the battle's storm;
So proud his glance, so glad her smile,
   With their happy friends beside them;
It seem'd that earth or earthly guile
   Might ne'er again divide them.

" Dear maiden, art thou ready now?"
　　Thus gently spake the man of God.
The blushing cheek, the calm, sweet brow,
　　Proclaimed the power of Cupid's rod;
But ah! there's naught on earth secure!
　　E'en love itself is sad and brief;
The bright young life, the good and pure,
　　Are dying like the autumn leaf.

The missile dread rush'd through the air;
　　It burst upon the peaceful scene;
The lovely girl, so brave, so fair,
　　Show'd death upon her virgin mien;
And while with sobs the rites were spoke,
　　That he his bride might there possess,
She struggled ere her spirit broke,
　　And e'en in dying answered, "Yes."

Many a story's writ in gold
　　Of withered hopes and broken bliss,
But bard nor minstrel ne'er hath told
　　A nobler, sadder one than this.
Then strike the lyre's most mournful strings
　　To music's soft and soothing tone!
Let sorrow ope her chast'ning wings
　　For her that's gone, and him that's lone!

O, daughters of the dear Southland!
　　Embalm with tears your sister's fate!
'Twill whet her soldier husband's brand,
　　And soften, too, his bitter hate;
For surely on the red, dun field,
　　Though cannon sweep the plain with fire,
Her angel soul will be his shield,
　　And mercy's smile will change his ire.

But not alone will shadows deep
   O'ercast the face of Southland's maids;
Columbia's daughters all will weep
   That one so true so early fades;
And beauty's voice in every clime,
   Though he by some is unforgiven,
Will sighing chant a dirge sublime
   For her who thus has passed to heav'n!

WHAT IS HEAVEN?

[My friend, General Thompson, has asked me, " What is heaven? " saying that I thought it " a Methodist camp-meeting." I answer, I know not, but the Bible teaches us that " eye hath not seen, ear hath not heard, neither hath it entered into the heart of man to conceive " of it.]

OH, a wonderful place that heaven must be,
   Which thrills all men with hopes so profound,
And often we think, when the fancy is free,
Of the happified ones who've passed us to see
   Where that city, so lovely, is found.

No mortal can paint the ineffable shore
   Which skirteth the boundary of time,
Nor picture the pleasures of those gone before,
Whose yearnings and heart-aches forever are o'er,
   In the bliss of that glorified clime.

Millions of beings, all radiant and bright,
   For whom was blood in agony shed,
Are casting their gems, with seraphic delight,
At the feet of the Prince whose mercy and might
   Brought crowns of life to honor each head.

No passion that's earthly polluteth the heart,
    No cares distract when safe at the goal ;
No pangs of remorse or repentance shall smart,
Nor thorns in the flesh shall their sorrows impart,
    To war against the rest of the soul.

But ever and ever, as years roll apace,
    Number'd alone in the cycles above,
Shall knowledge and virtue increase ev'ry grace,
And glory enkindle the celestial face,
    Reflecting the truth that God is love.

Fort Delaware, 1864.

A PRAYER.

Let me, O Lord, thy mercy prove;
Yea, feel thy never-dying love,
And my poor soul for realms above
    Be ready, waiting evermore;
So when the angel shall proclaim
That even Time must change his name,*
And worlds on worlds are wrapped in flame,
    I'll meet thee on the heav'nly shore!

THE PICTURE IN MY PHOTOGRAPHIC ALBUM.

There is a picture in my book
    Which smiles upon me day by day,
Yet, though there's language in each look,
    It never has a word to say;

---

* Time will be swallowed up by eternity.

And every secret of this heart
  This silent one is getting now,
Which sometimes makes me sudden start,
  For 'tis a woman's lovely brow.

Each night, each morn I gaze again,
  To see if change is written there,
But still the picture soothes each pain
  While looking on the face so fair;
And then I think a bosom warm
  With life and hope and love-lit flame
Is beating now with many a charm
  From whence this quiet picture came.

And then regretful thoughts will come
  That this is all I e'er may see;
That ne'er, within her happy home,
  Her real face will beam on me.
But what of that?—she knows me not;
  My very name to her's unknown;
Nor does she even know the spot,
  The mountain land I call my own.

But, O, there is a heart doth beat
  And chafe for him who's gone away,
And little Jimmie prattles sweet
  About his own, his dear "Papa."
Keep back, ye tears—ye must not fall;
  Stern manhood bids ye cease to flow;
Our God, our homes, our country all
  Proclaim that none must yield to woe.

Fort Delaware, 1864.

THE ROSE.

[On receiving a beautifully embellished volume of poems from
Miss Rose G., of Baltimore, Md.]

There's not a flower or pretty thing
    That in the garden grows
On which the bee can rest its wing
    That's equal to the rose.
Each morn unfolds its velvet leaves
    To catch the falling dew,
And 'round its stem fond Cupid weaves
    His web for bosoms true,
And ties the golden knot of love
    With such a happy string
That all the Cupids from above
    Light on the 'trothal ring.
Then bloom for aye, fair, gentle Rose,
    While loving hearts are given,
Till ev'ry breast with pleasure glows
    Akin to that in heaven.

Fort Delaware, 1864.

TO LIEUTENANT S., A FELLOW-PRISONER.

When years are gone and war is o'er,
And hostile hosts shall meet no more
With musket bright and pointed spear
To try the nerve and shock the ear;
When peace with robe of light hath come
To bless again each Southland home;
When brooks and rills and mountain dells
Shall catch the echo as it swells,
And hill and vale and smiling plain
Shall shout to hear the happy strain;

When flocks and herds shall quiet graze
Through all the pleasant summer days,
And lambs shall gambol light and free
When birds give forth their minstrelsy;
When gather'd 'round our hearths we are,
And wife and babes our bliss do share,
And love shall raise its beaming eye
To Him, our Father, in the sky;
Then fancy, tireless, o'er the main
Will bring us to these scenes again.
When by our our sides the good wife sits,
And on the hearth the bright blaze flits;
When Jimmie climbs his father's knee
To pull his beard with childish glee,
And, while without doth fly the gale,   •
Says, "Papa, tell your boy a tale;"
Then fields of fight shall rise anew,
When cannon peal'd and minies flew,
And victors' shouts were sad allied
With sighs and groans from those who died;
Then prison days shall, too, appear
Before the eyes of those who hear,
And flowing tears shall wet the cheek
With thanks, too deep for words to speak,
That all is past, the conflict done,
The battle fought, the vict'ry won.

Fort Delaware, 1864.

DO THEY MISS ME AT HOME?

Do they miss me at home? I often ask,
  As the wearisome hours are passing by,
When the Northman's chain and the Northman's task
  Are impaling me here, perhaps to die.

Do they miss me there where long, long ago
    The earth to me was so cheering and bright;
Where life's young morn did encha tingly glow
    With visions of beauty ever in sight?

Do they miss me at home since autumn's breath
    Hath color'd the woods and scatter'd the leaves,
And the beauteous flowers have pal'd in death
    Where but late they stood in their fragrant sheaves?
Do they miss me there since the birds are gone
    That so sweetly sang in the cherry trees,
And soft music made as the day wore on
    With their tinier friends, the busy bees?

Do they miss me at home when twilight gray
    Hath mantled the world in its sable hue;
When the peafowl screams on the hill away,
    And the guineas are roosting in the yew;
When homeward the plowboy taketh his way,
    All glad in his heart for his work is done,
And beautiful then o'er the dying day
    The bright stars come out, even one by one?

Do they miss me at home when on the board
    The linen is spread and the meal is laid;
When the joyous word which the heart doth hoard
    By each one around is so sweetly said;
When mother's dear face is seen at the head,
    If still she's alive to cherish her child,
Though her raven hair has a silvery thread
    Adorning a brow still gentle and mild?

Do they miss me at home when 'round the fire
    The wee ones do frolic with winsome glee;
When all then are present but him—their sire—
    To join in the sport so happy and free;

When fondly the wife and mother doth smile
  On each little head that's passing in view,
The prayer in her soul that naught may beguile
  Their innocent feet from ways that are true?

Do they miss me at home, that precious throng,
  When the hallow'd hour of prayer draws nigh;
When lifted above the melodious song .
  Is given in praise to Him in the sky;
When the dear old Bible upon the stand
  Is open'd and read with reverent awe,
And blessing is sought for all in the band
  To guide them aright in keeping the law?

Do they miss me at home when Sabbath bells
  Are chiming their messages in the air,
And ever each note so pleasingly tells
  "There's room for ye all in the house of prayer;"
When pastor and flock are wending their way
  To the church as it stands upon the hill,
And meekly they bow when they hear him say,
  "The Lord's in his temple—let earth be still?"

Can ye tell, ye winds that so wildly flee
  From the mountain peak o'er the hill and plain,
What tidings from home, the land of the free,
  Ye bear to the captive to cheer him again?
Can ye speak no word in your fierce career
  Of their state and health as ye swift flew on?
Did they miss me at home—ah! did the tear
  Fall sad on the ground for the absent one?

Yes! thanks be to God! they miss me at home;
  I feel it e'en now in my heart's deep core;
And fond ones repeat, "When, when will he come,
  To stray from his home and his friends no more?"

Then, cheer thee, sad soul, in this weary breast
   The blessing ye need will come at the last;
Kind Heaven will give thee the happiest rest
   When these dreary days forever are past.

Fort Delaware, 1864.

LINES FOR A LADY'S ALBUM.

THIS book is clean and pure and beautiful;
   No stain is resting on its swan-like sheets,
Reminding us both that the dutiful
   And pure are those whom highest pleasure greets.

In your friendship, delicate and tender,
   You have requested me to place my name
First on these snowy pages, and render
   You a pleasure, which is my fervent aim.

Ne'er did soldier, thirsting deep for glory,
   Or pilgrim kneeling at a holy shrine,
Feel warmer hope than I that my story
   May be pure as this book—my thoughts as thine.

I would write some word of deathless beauty
   In this thy book, my faithful, gentle friend—
Some word to cheer in life's every duty
   Whose far-reaching attraction ne'er shall end.

How wondrous is the thought! in the regions
   Of God's galaxy of worlds, in the sky,
Each star amid the myriad legions
   Attracts the others in their paths on high.

Let me, ere I write, delay and ponder
   What word of love may be for thee the best
As along life's stream your feet may wander,
   Seeking ever there a haven full of rest.

A thousand streams of joy and love and gladness
　Come gliding in between the rocks and hills,
And, though often fleck'd with gloom and sadness,
　They fill the heart with sweet and precious thrills.

We cannot safely build below God's heaven,
　Because the rainbow's form, alas! will fade,
And every tint which to the rose is given
　Will leave a grief when they have all decayed.

Dear friend, life is always in our keeping;
　We wisely act when we shall seek the true;
For e'en when the soul itself is weeping
　'Twill teach us how to live and how to do.

I need not tell you all.　The deep quiver
　Of the soul before its God is that thy peace
On either side of Life's tree and river
　May be with Him with whom all pain shall cease.

Last night of Forty-eighth Congress.

DARLING.

I'm all alone, my darling, in the room
　Where thou gavest me the last kiss of earth,
And strive to think amid my tears and gloom
　If I can tell thy true and priceless worth.
Long since thou camest from thy mountain home
　With trust, and thy tender heart did quiver,
As, passing near Mount Mitchell's mighty dome,
　We joyful came to the racing river *
In dear old Buncombe, whose bright waters come

---

* The French Broad.

4

From the mountain peaks where the wild beasts
    roam.
The bloom of the peach was on thy cheek, dear,
  And thy step as light as the timid fawn's
Among the wooded hills, afar and near,
    When first the rosy tint of morning dawns
    Upon the groves, the flowers, and pleasant lawns.
'God blessed us, darling, in our early morn,
  And gave us much of hope and love to see
As loving children unto us were born;
    And our home was glad with joy as the wee
    Toddlers filled all the house with mirth and glee—
The happiest sight which on the earth may be.
But ah, I do remember keenly now
  When first I saw thy step begin to fail,
And marked upon thy precious, snowy brow,
    The sign of that which made my heart to quail
And bosom beat with its own terror pale.
    Then came the watching and the aching fears,
The constant dread, the shortening of the breath,
  The hectic flush, the eyes too bright for tears;
And thou wert claimed, alas! my love, by death,
  Giving us the grief, thou the Christian's wreath.
Now, in the silent watches of the night,
  I call for thee, dear partner of my life,
But miss thy loved form, and the beaming light
  Of thy sweet face, which as mother and wife
Shone on us all, so good, so pure, so bright.
  Never more, O never more will we hear
Thy sweet voice in song, at dear Riverside,
  Thrilling us with its tones, as pure and clear
As the streamlet's song, where the waters glide
To music, seeking ocean's moving tide.

We cannot call thee back to us again,
   Love, for thou art gone to that far-off bourn
   Whence "no traveler returns," leaving us to mourn
Our irreparable loss.   The joy or pain
   Of earth cannot break or mar thy deep rest
In "the land of the leal," where every strain
   Of joy bursts from radiant throngs, who, dressed
In Jesus' robes of spotless white, on plain
   And hill of the restful country, are blest
With peace, and love, and joy without a stain.
   But, God be praised! if we but love the Lord
   And walk obedient to his holy word,
We'll go to thee when life and earth are done,
And, darling, there we'll be forever one.

Washington City, 911 Rhode Island Avenue, 1886.

RIZPAH.

"And Rizpah the daughter of Aiah took sackcloth, and spread it for her upon the rock, from the beginning of harvest until water dropped upon them out of heaven, and suffered neither the birds of the air to rest upon them by day, nor the beasts of the field by night." (2 Samuel xxi. 10.)

SAUL had stood in majesty in the field
   Of a fearful battle.   O'er the people,
In shining armor, bearing a sword and shield
   Of ponderous weight, like some tall steeple
He towered; from the shoulders upward his form
   Was far above the mightiest; his locks,
From under his helmet, in the fierce storm
   Of battle waved like billows on the rocks
When the earth receives the wild ocean shocks.

Before the closing of that mournful day,
    Mournful to God's afflicted people, the King,
Deserted by his Maker, afraid to pray,
    Was dark in soul, a miserable thing,
    With not a hope to which his soul could cling.
The beaded sweat was on his forehead high,
    And his heart in keenest agony riven
When he saw no spot to which he could fly
    From the wrath of Jehovah; the dark heaven
    Gave no token that peace or help was nigh;
And O alas! before the setting sun
The Philistines their bloody work had done!

On Gilboa's lonely mount the wretched King
    Beheld his army beaten; his brave son,
The princely Jonathan, whose strong bow-string
    Had never turned from the mighty, upon
Whose form of beauty Israel's fair maids
Had gazed with joy, arranging the dark braids
    Of their glossy hair to catch his bright eye—
    Alas, that one so full of love should die!—
Was wrapped in his bloody garments, his sword
    Beside his flaming shield and his bare head,
Resting on the holy soil which the Lord
    In mercy gave the tribes he thither led.
And now King Saul, in that most awful hour,
    Was sorely pressed upon the rugged height
    Of Mount Gilboa; the grandeur of his might
And all the emblems of his royal power
    Were fading forever from his anxious sight,
While 'round him there Elohim's wrath did lower;
    No hope had he on earth—none with his God;
    So, dying there, he rested on the sod.

King David rested from his stubborn fight
   With those who came to spoil the place, Ziklag,
In which he met them in his valiant might,
And smote them hip and thigh from evening light
   To eventide again; nor did they flag
In fight till they destroyed the Amalekite.
   But as he rested, one from the camp of Saul,
With his clothes rent and earth upon his head,
   Cast o'er the King and those around the pall
Of a great sorrow, saying, "Saul is dead."
   Then the King, the Psalmist of Israel,
   Broke forth in song his royal woe to tell:

" The beauty of Israel is slain,
  Upon thy high places it is gone.
   How are the mighty fallen!
Tell it not in Gath nor Askelon,
Lest the daughters of the Philistines rejoice.
On Gilboa's mountains let there be no dew,
Nor rain, nor fields of offerings,
For there the shield of the mighty away
Was cast, as though the King was not anointed.
From the blood of the slain in battle,
From the terrible power of the mighty,
The bow of Jonathan turned not back,
Nor the sword of Saul to the scabbard empty.
Saul and Jonathan were lovely in life,
And in death they still were undivided:
Swifter they than eagles, stronger than lions.

" Daughters of Israel, weep over Saul;
He clothed you with scarlet and gave delights;
He put ornaments of gold on your apparel.
  How are the mighty fallen!

In the midst of the battle, O Jonathan,
Thou wast slain in thine high places.
I am distressed for thee, Jonathan,
My brother; pleasant thou hast been to me;
Thy love to me, my brother, was wonderful,
Passing even the love of woman.
    How are the mighty fallen!
The weapons of war, alas! have perished."

The famine was sore in Israel.   Year
    By year, for three years, the Lord was in wrath
Because King Saul had stained his warlike spear
    With the blood of Gibeon, that from his path
He might sweep them from the earth, though they'd
        sworn
That not a soul should from them e'er be torn.
    Then David said to Gibeon, "What wish
    Have you because of Saul, the son of Kish?"
"Seven sons of Saul," was their determined word,
"That we may hang them all before the Lord."
    The King delivered Saul's unhappy sons
    To these unrelenting and cruel ones;
And when the barley harvest-time drew nigh,
    They took these children of their once mighty
        chief,
And brought them to Gibeah, there to die,
    And leave poor Rizpah in her matchless grief.

There on the rock, in that sad harvest-time,
    The heroic woman the sackcloth spread
For herself, that she might with love sublime
    Watch o'er the bodies of her blameless dead,
And drive away the carrion birds by day,
And keep the night beasts from their hapless prey.

No rest for Rizpah, neither day nor night,
But with devotion rare to any given,
   Without complaint, but with a mother's pain,
She watched her boys—O, what a holy sight!—
Till God, from out the gentle, loving heaven,
   Gave her the sweet and happy sound of rain.

Let Homer sound his harp once more,
Search every land from shore to shore;
   Heroic Greece, and valiant Rome,
   And capitols from base to dome;
In England's land, and Scotia's hills,
And France, where love of glory thrills;
   The Western World, where Freedom s song
   Hath beauty given to right o'er wrong;
And every spot on God's green earth
Where true devotion has had birth;
   But never, never will there be
   A sweeter story told to thee.

King David, the man after God's own heart,
   Was told of Rizpah's wondrous, faithful love,
And in the burial of the dead took part,
   As well became a man esteemed above;
And when 'twas done at his own free command,
The Lord was asked to bless his chosen land.

1886.

———

THE STAR.*

ONE quiet eve—I may not tell thee when—
   As after toil upon my bed reclining,
I saw what I have never seen since then—
   A sweet star upon me softly shining.

---

* L'homme propose, et Dieu dispose.

It was through the window light I saw it,
 Serene in all its loveliness and beauty,
And my soul was energized to draw it,
 That it might shine along my path of duty.

But O! fond dream—it was too far away
 Among the starry worlds which o'er us glitter
To heed my cry, yet still it seemed to say,
 "Go on alone to meet life's sweet and bitter."

Long then I gazed upon it that lone night,
 Though never once its coldness there upbraided,
Till down the sky its sweet and mellow light
 From my sad heart and view forever faded.

But O! when it was truly from me gone,
 No heed it giving to my earnest calling,
It seemed as if the day would never dawn,
 The darkness was so dense and so appalling.

And often now I turn my anxious eye
 Toward the spot where last I saw it beaming,
Amid the orbs along the far-off sky,
 And hope, in truth, that I am only dreaming.

But day by day the outlook is the same,
 Nor sky nor star give me the faintest token
That ever here I may the favor claim
 Of its sweet light upon a hope that's broken.

Ah! sometimes on the toilsome road of life
 There comes a star across the bosom's vision
Which with the sweetest, fondest things is rife,
 And on the heart it makes such deep incision

That time, nor space, nor grief, nor aching woe,
 Though seemingly the strong affections killing,

Can ever on earth cause it to forego
 The dear memories of a thing so thrilling.

But I am like the lone and blasted pine
 Upon the silent and the rugged mountain,
Around whose form there never more may twine
 The gentle vine, fed by the snowy fountain.

Nor should I grieve, for soon the end will be;
 Nor find it question for the soul's debating;
For o'er the borders of eternity
 My precious ones for me are anxious waiting.

I hear from on the river's further verge
 Their words of joy, their songs of love and won-
  der;
The invitations which they sweetly urge
 To come, that we no longer be asunder.

And O, my darlings, to your peaceful home
 My steps, my heart, my soul, my life are tending
With rapture for the glory yet to come,
 Where love, and peace, and rest, and bliss are
  blending.

TO MISS KATE.

[When she was starting from Washington to Canada.]

Two ladies sat in easy chairs
 One summer day in '84,
Whose charming persons, pleasing airs
 Beguiled the man within the door.

The one was maiden in her bloom,
 With gentle eye and blushing face,

And step as light as heron's plume,
   And every motion was a grace.

The other's brow and queenly form
   Were 'circled with that sphere of life
Which woman's love with worship warm
   Adorns as mother and as wife.

" Write in my book," the maiden said,
   With low, soft voice and winning smile,
" Before my feet are homeward sped
   O'er hill and brake for many a mile."

Then spake the matron tenderly—
   Her thoughts along the steam steed's track:
" Write in her book this quest for me—
   ' My darling Katie, hasten back.' "

Ah! will she come?   In her own land
   Perchance some noble youth may dwell,
The lightest touch of whose loved hand
   May cause her virgin heart to swell.

If this be true, no chiding word
   Must from our aching souls be prest,
For well we know our bonny bird
   Must surely have her own sweet nest.

If wing and breast and heart be free,
   Which much we doubt, alack! alack!
Then let her eye this city see,
   And "darling Katie" hasten back.

Let flood, nor stream, nor crowded street,
   Nor city spire, nor sylvan charms
Delay nor check her flying feet
   Till she is in her friend's true arms,

DEAR MOTHER, ART THOU STANDING NEAR?

[Written the night before Christmas, 1864, at Fort Delaware.]

DEAR Mother, art thou standing near?
    Is this thy form before me now?
Is this indeed a mother's tear
    Upon my head and on my brow?
If 'tis thy form, O let me kneel
    And be again thy baby b y,
That this poor heart once more may feel
    The thrilling gush of childish joy!

And, Mother, shall I hang to-night
    My stocking in the same old place,
And will Saint Nicholas alight
    And show to me his smiling face?
And shall I hear his tiny steeds
    Upon the chimney's smoking top,
As, bent upon his happy deeds,
    He from the roof shall nimbly hop?

And, Mother, will the stocking hold
    The butternuts and raisins fair;
The candy sticks and hearts of gold,
    The fairies with their shining hair?
And shall I find the plume and cap,
    The little sword and soldier boots
With which, while in their Christmas nap,
    Dear Santa Claus the children suits?

And, Mother, when the morning light
    Shall speak another Christmas come,
Will thy dear features be as bright
    As when they graced my boyhood's home?

And wilt thou smile as fondly still
  When "Christmas-gift" is prattling said,
And seek to charm my childish will
  With pretty toys of blue and red?

And wilt thou tell me of His charms—
  Good Mary's babe, the infant Lord—
Who lay within His mother's arms,
  According to the angel's word?
And, Mother, may I go again
  To see Him in the manger laid,
Where Magi from the star-lit plain
  Their gifts of gold and spices made?

And, Mother, wilt thou let me lean
  My weary head upon thy breast,
That my fond spirit still may glean
  Sweet comfort from that place of rest?
And let me dream—ah, fondly dream—
  That childhood's hour again is giv'n;
And, though 'tis but a passing gleam,
  I'll hope to find it true in heav'n.

ASTORIA.

[Written for the Author's faithful friends, the Fosters.]

LIFE is not all tears.   There be sunny slopes
  And sweetly gliding streams and smiling plains
To break its rugged aspect, though the hopes
  Of youth may have perished in the sad pains
Of disappointment, fading, as it were,
  Like the flowers i' the early spring-time;
Though the angel of childhood may nowhere
  Bless the anxious eye with the sweep sublime

Of her radiant wings, filling the soul
　With pleasures unspeakable; though lone tears
May come from the heart's deep fountain, and roll
　O'er the care-worn face, saying that the years
Of peaceful glee will come no more; yet, O,
　The welcome kind, the sympathizing word
And gentle smile wring gladness out of woe,
　And leave the heart like some free, happy bird.
　　　Belov'd Astoria! 'Tis surely strange
That in the din, the rush, the madden'd hour
Of this most selfish world, so full of change
　Thy scenes should hold with such a pleasing pow'r
The heart of him who writes. Scarce twenty days
　Have thrown their light across the field and glen
Since first he heard thy sweet, euphonious name;
　And scarce so many hours have fled since when
With all a soldier's ardor, he did gaze
　Upon the forms of those who went and came
Within thy peaceful walks, and yet, and yet,
　Thou'rt now a well-spring of joy gushing up,
Destined still to grow till life's sun shall set,
　A sweeten'd draught—in life's most bitter cup.

War Time, 1865.

TO A BOUQUET.

SWEET flowers! Ye touch a tender chord
　Within my bosom's inmost core,
And in your gentle language speak
　Of days and hours which come no more;
The glad, gay hours of early life
　Spent in my sunny, mountain home,
To me the dearest resting-place
　This side the heav'n's eternal dome.

'Twas in those hours in that fair land,
   On many a cliff of lofty height,
I first beheld your sisters' bloom,
   And pluck'd them with a wild delight,
And brought them from the mountain's brow
   With all a brother's tender care
To one who watches now for me,
   And twin'd them in her dark brown hair.

I loved them then, I love ye now,
   Though years on years have fled away,
And catch with joy the fragrant breath
   From out your cups and leaflets gay.
And yet methinks 'twere best to own -
   That ye posse-s a charm more sweet
Because my friend's kind hand hath borne
   Ye from your lovely native seat.

And will ye not in quiet tones
   Proclaim to her that every deed
Of kindness to the suffering shown
   Will wreathe for her a fadeless meed—
That ev'ry word in kindness said,
   And ev'ry faithful prayer thus giv'n,
Will give new flowers to many a heart,
   And bud and bloom for her in heav'n?

New York City, 1865.

RICHMOND ON THE JAMES.

A CAPTIVE of the "Stonewall Corps" at grim Fort Delaware,
Where none might feel dear woman's touch or hear her
   fervent pray'r,

Was giving up his bright young life, the hopes which
    bless'd his birth,
The cause he truly had at heart, and all he lov'd on earth,
When, as his comrades stood around with sad and droop-
    ing eyes,
And gazed upon the wasted form, no more on earth to rise,
He murmur'd of the absent ones and call'd beloved names,
Then fondly spoke of Richmond—his Richmond on the
    James:

"I mourn for thee, lov'd city, since now thy strength is
    low,
And o'er thee waves so haughtily the banner of the foe,
And many a stately building's gone where fond the eye
    did rest,
And many a stricken family with house nor home are blest;
But even as my heart doth break there comes this sooth-
    ing thought,
Thy children for their country bled—they have not died
    for naught—
Thy suff'rings and thy valor tried, thy heroes and thy
    dames
Shall gild fore'er the story of Richmond on the James.

" E'en now I see my childhood friends, as on the smooth,
    green hill
We played beneath the giant oaks close by a silver rill;
And hark! I hear again the shout, the boyish, glad huzza
From bands who gaily bounc'd the ball or handled well
    the taw;
And ne'er did happier music ring along the greenwood
    wild
Than came from out the joyous throat of many a guileless
    child.

The very sunlight seem'd to smile upon our merry games,
But we'll play no more at Ri hmond—lov'd Richmond on
  the James.

"And evermore there is a form before this failing eye—
My mother blesses still her boy each time she's passing by.
Her latest kiss is on my lip, which none hath kiss'd away,
Though she nor I did think 'twould last until my dying
  day;
And as my life is ebbing fast, 'tis sure a grateful thing
For me to tell how miserly I to her love do cling.
And well I may—'twas her dear self who taught me life's
  best aims
On her honor'd knees at Richmond—dear Richmond on
  the James.

"And sister, too, is by my bed—how co ld we be apart,
Since in the peaceful days gone by I liv'd within her heart?
And did she not with her own hand give me my father's
  sword,
And whisper with a glowing cheek the gallant, noble
  word—
'Go, brother, go; your comrades stand upon Virginia's
  shore,
While "Lee and Stonewall" both are there to face the bat-
  tle's roar?'
And yet I fear since that proud day she oft her ardor
  blames;
But she did it all for Richmond—brave Richmond on the
  James.

"And bend your heads, my comrades true; your faces all
  bring near,
And do not wonder if my e'e gives forth its last, last tear.
A vision comes before me now of loveliness and truth—

'Tis my Anna! 'tis my Anna! in all her witching youth!
We grew together as children, and heart was knit to heart,
And I was aye the happy lad who took the maiden's part;
And both at last that love did own which the wild spirit
    tames,
But I'll woo no mere at Richmond—sweet Richmond on
    the James.

"Yes, you'll tell them I am dying, and what the soldier
    said,
And where my jailer carelessly shall lay their darling's
    head.
Too many tears they must not drop o'er this my mournful
    doom,
Though some should even seek to carve 'A Traitor' on my
    tomb;
And, though no woman's fingers white may twine the
    roses there,
Nor Fame for me a laurel wreathe, both beautiful and fair,
Little I'll reck, little I'll care if I shall ne'er be Fame's,
So they take my dust to Richmond—my Richmond on the
    James."

His head fell back, his eye grew dim, the warm heart
    ceased to beat,
And the youthful soldier slumber'd in rest both long and
    sweet,
While o'er his brow, by suff'ring worn, as the last blow
    was giv'n,
There came the calm and peaceful look which comes alone
    from heav'n.
Then, sorrowful, they turn'd away, his comrades one and
    all,
As stranger hands did bear him thence beneath his hum-
    ble pall;

5

Nor ever have they seen the spot, upon the river's verge,
Where by his grave the breakers make a melancholy dirge.

But still they hope, when after years have calm'd the
    hearts of men,
And Peace has spread her snowy robe o'er mountain, vale,
    and glen,
And never more shall war's alarms spread terror and dis-
    may
From city, town, and hamlet rude to many a cot away;
When kinder words than now are spoke shall of the South
    be said,
Nor libels vile, nor falsehoods sheer by prejudice be read;
Yea, even when all hate is gone, and love shall light its
    flames,
To carry his dust to Richmond—our Richmond on the
    James.

    Fort Delaware, 1865.

MY LOVE.

My love lies hidden in my heart,
    But still within my eye;
Though unkind fate doth keep us part,
    Sweet fancy brings her nigh.

My ear is thrilled with her dear step,
    A step as light as dew,
When o'er my soul blest dreams have crept,
    Entrancing, kind, and true.

Through all the watches of the night,
    When 'round the sleeping world
God hangs his banner'd hosts so bright,
    As onward they are whirled,

Delicious visions of her form
   Float through the liquid air,
And I can feel her breathing warm,
   Though only fancy's there.

The dear, dear head comes gently down
   Upon my breast to rest,
While the rich lacing of her gown
   Against my heart is prest.

And o'er and o'er I count each hair
   With rapture never told,
Nor would I change with fortune's heir
   A single one for gold.

The mild, blue eye looks in my face
   And answers back each glance,
And in each sparkle I can trace
   What doth my breast entrance.

The precious mouth, the ruby lips
   Close tenderly on mine,
And while the soul its nectar sips
   The heart has bliss divine.

The modest face is all aglow
   With tenderness and love,
And beauteous blushes come and go,
   Her innocence to prove.

Ah, me! how truly and how well
   Do I God's image trace
In the glad magic of the spell
   That's in my darling's face!

THE STEP UPON THE STAIR.

[Lines on receiving a visit from a lady while the writer was
quite ill.]

ONE night, while silence in the house was deep,
  And I was passing into dreaming,
Just half awake, and only half asleep,
  In each condition only seeming,

I heard a step upon the winding stair
  As light as dew-drops on the river,
Or thistledown in summer's balmy air,
  Where zephyrs 'mid the roses quiver.

I listened till it gently moved again,
  As if a work it must deliver—
A woman's work—to soothe a brow of pain,
  And give a blessing like the giver.

That step still lingers on my listening ear,
  A sound to be forgotten never;
My heart says, soft, its sweet impression's here
  To live forever and forever.

THE BROKEN TESSERA.

THERE were two. One was young, and grave, and fair;
  Her brow, whiter than snow, was lifted up
With a wealth of brain, while her glossy hair
  Waved 'round its polished surface, and the cup
Of her beauty seemed full in its deep black.
  Each wave of the jetty braids, which he loved
With all the ardor of a quenchless joy,
  Filled his soul with new longings, giving him back

With tumultuous bounds—no trifling toy—
  A sweeter hope than ever earth had proved.
Her red lips, like ripe fruit on the bough,
  Clos'd gently o'er the shining ivory,
Seeming to say to the rapt gazer, " Come, n w,
  And touch, and taste, and drink to ecstasy."
Her form—ah, that was queenly to the eye
  Of the other—tall, graceful, lithe, erect,
Fashioned with an art so grand and so high
  That only one—heaven's great Architect—
Did mold it in its likeness to the sky.
  Her mind was clear, strong, and truly gentle,
Catching at once the beautiful and true
  Which glow in the physical and mental,
Whether on earth, or sea, or heaven's deep blue.
  Her kind heart was brimmed with gentlest mercy,
Such as angels feel while they are keeping
  Watch o'er suffering; not, indeed, the hearsay
Mercy of books, but such as, ne'er sleeping,
Lives in deeds, the golden harvest reaping.
The other one was neither young nor fair,
  Nor fame, nor wealth, nor pride, nor grandeur his,
For time had silvered o'er his own dark hair,
  And left him, in its flight, just simply this:
A man whose soul was warm with love and hope;
  Whose eye was glad to see fair nature's dress;
Whose heart took in the beatific scope
  Of things that in their holy work would b'ess;
Whose heart was ever in his open hand;
  Nor child, nor maid, nor man need shun with fear
His steps—for all from him within his land
  Met this: In joy, a smile ; in grief, a tear.
And thus they met.   Upon her blameless life

And maiden hope, and dream of purest bliss,
Had fallen disappointment's blight.   The keen knife
   Of despair cut the rootlets of her soul,
And she hungered for a fond one's true kiss,
   Deeming true love on earth her long-sought goal.
In agony she cried to him for love,
   This one so framed for love, to her denied;
And nestling to him, like a wounded dove,
   She sought his heart there resting by his side.
He gave her love; from his own being
   He drew a deep and ever-blissful tide,
Which caused his full breast to dream of seeing
   Joy in this world, with hope for his fair bride.
Then in that glad hour, when their souls were knit
   Into one joyous seam of love, they drank
The cup of rapture; and oft did they sit
   Silent, happy, deeming earth was not blank.
Then 'round her swan-like throat, her snowy neck,
   He linked a chain of gold, a tiny chain,
With a token, the face of which no speck
   Of sin might stain, or aught that bringeth pain.
In the bright circle a single word was writ—
" Lead us not into temptation," under it.
     Thus they parted.   .   .   .   .
   When once again they met, all joy was gone,
All hope was dead save one—a blessed hope—
   That as the years were passing, passing on,
They both might see the sacred city's slope;
   They both might catch the far-off angel song,
And lift their eyes to that eternal rest
   Where Jesus keeps his holy, happy throng,
And in his bosom they are ever blest.
   With streaming eyes she laid the dead token

At his feet—poor Magdalene!—said, " Forgive,"
  And watched him as, with his heart all broken,
He sadly kissed it, forgave, and bade her live.

   .   .   .   .

  She is gone and he is left.   Never more
  This side life's outermost and boundless shore
  Shall lip and brow between these loved ones meet
  In fond embrace and in communion sweet.
  Their paths have parted on this weary strand,
  And each looks to the Savior's good red hand
  To guide them to the peaceful home above,
  Where all is perfect tenderness and love.

LITTLE WILLIE.

[Willie lived on Riverside Farm, North Carolina.]

DID you know little Willie?   On the bank
  Of the river, our own beloved river,
Where gentle violets grew, he first drank
  The joys of life, sent him by life's Giver.
In the waters of the sweet stream he saw
  The play of the fishes as their sharp fins
Cut the clear waves, and knew the wise law
  Of their kind keeps them where their life begins
The world to him was beautiful.   The peak
  Of the great mountain resting near the sky,
Which there doth catch the sun's first crimson streak,
  As rising from its bed it flames on high,
Was gay with trees, and birds, and tiny flowers,
Children of God, which gladdened nature's bowers—
  Those he loved.   His young, tender soul was full

Of the song of the robin, the squirrel's bark,
  And the soft coo of the sweet dove; no lull
Of joy for him, because he heard the lark.
  From the mighty hills he watched the clouds
Flying in heaven, forming thunder-heads,
  And gazed with awe upon the shadowy shrouds
Which by us glide when the earth with heaven weds.
  Thus Willie lived.   Gentle, and meek, and mild,
He kindly spoke to every passing one,
  Giving his mother joy in her dear child,
Till e'en toil was sweet if for him 'twas done.

.   .   .   .

One winter day a stranger at the gate
  Alighted from a pale and shaggy steed,
And stamped the ground, as if he would not wait
  An answer to his knock, because of greed
  To rob the flock and make their bosoms bleed.
Tall, and gaunt, and grim, his unbidden form
  Crossed not alone above the humble sill
Of that modest threshold; in calm, in storm,
  O'er earth, on ocean, plain, and lonely hill,
In frozen lands, or in the tropics warm,
  At every hour, the rider, by his will,
  Pressed on his steed as if his maw to fill.

A thousand battle-fields had been to him
  A carnival of joy, as the squadrons swept
The plain with sword and spear in the fierce vim
  Of the deadly struggle, where glory kept
  Crowns for heroes, forgetting those who wept.
Before the Christ had offered earth his peace,
  This insatiate one, on his pale horse,

Had with the Roman legions charged; no cease
  Of his greed on Arbela's plain, though corse
And beast were low before the pride of Greece.
  No human power could stay this dreadful one,
For he had no pity.   He struck the child,
  The lonely widow's only hope—her son—
And naught of earth has ever yet beguiled
This rider and his steed so pale and wild,
  As still he whets his keen and fatal scythe,
And hurls his darts on high; the swift arrow
  Of his hate sparing not the sad, the blithe,
Nor the feeble—the foe of e'en the sparrow.

So at the door with dire alarm and dread
  We speechless stood, as if we there could push
The gaunt fiend from sick Willie's trundle-bed,
  And drive him out into the night's deep hush,
  Or to the river where the waters rush.
But O, not all our cries and bitter tears,
  Our anguished hearts, where affection lingers
So fondly, could mitigate our sad fears,
  Or keep dear Willie from death's cold fingers!

.   .   .   .

If you will go with me upon some eve,
  In this the month of May, I'll show you where
We laid the little form, and had to leave
  It till Jesus comes with angels in the air.

No stone is there to mark the resting-place
  Of the pale boy, but I could joyful see
On another, through the tears upon my face,
  "Suffer little children to come unto me."

PASSING, PASSING.

[Written on a postal card aboard of the fast-mail train going South.]

Our life is like a mountain stream,
  Whose surging waters know no rest;
By hill and plain they flash and gleam
  Till gather'd on the ocean's breast.

Sometimes in calm, sometimes in storm,
  . Now white with wrath, now fleck'd with foam,
Then, imag'd in the rainbow's form,
  They onward move to find a home.

Sometimes their song is sweet and low,
  Sometimes 'tis sad, like funeral dirge;
And then they scarcely seem to go,
  But steal along the woodland verge.

But O, at length they shout with glee;
  Old ocean's roar breaks on each ear;
With joy they cry, "The sea! the sea!"
  Our rest will be forever here.

When lo! the sunbeam, swift and true,
  Shall kiss them from old Neptune's rod,
And fogs and mists, o'er fields of blue,
  Shall bear them back through clouds to God.

Such is our life, asleep, awake,
  Sometimes in smiles, sometimes in fears;
Sometimes sweet hope its flight shall take,
  And leave us pain, and grief, and tears.

Sometimes the heart beats low and faint,
  As troubles 'round our path increase,
And sin, and care, and earthly taint
  Hide from our view the bow of peace.

We look ahead and joyful greet
  Some "spot of green," just on before,
And fondly dream our tired feet
  Will nestle there forevermore.

Alas! when near the close of day
  We reach what seem'd the spot so fair,
We find it farther still away—
  Mirag'd upon the evening air.

This much we know: each pulse that beats,
  Each step we take beside the shore,
Each day, each hour the trav'ler greets
  Shall leave him less than were before.

So, when with us the day is done,
  When sight is dim, when life is past,
May God, through his beloved Son,
  Bring us to rest with him at last!

1882.

LITTLE MAGGIE'S DRESS.

Down by the foaming river's side
Sweet little Maggie did reside,
Who with her mother lived alone,
For all the rest were from them gone.
Two little brothers, sisters two
Had passed away from their fond view;
And Maggie's father, too, had passed
Across the stream which was his last,
And in a cabin mean and small,
Which held for them their little all,
The "wee bit" maid and mother gray
Dwelt just along the great highway.

And now 'twas near the picnic day
In the sweet and beauteous May,
Where all the children bright and gay
Were called to meet, and sing, and play;
But our Maggie, the tiny mite,
Though always joyous as a sprite,
Was standing now beside the road,
Her heart all heavy with a load,
Because she had no dress to wear
To meet the children going there,

When down the road a farmer came,
Who called her by her pretty name,
And said, " Ho, Maggie, tell me quick,
Are you going to the picnic?"
The little maiden dropped a tear,
And spoke a word into his ear,
Who never spoke another word,
But down the road his horse he spurred,
And sang aloud as on he went
About a friend whom God had sent.

Next eventide the man passed by,
But not a soul did greet his eye;
For Maggie and her mother, too,
While near at hand, were hid from view.
So, gently raising the door latch,
While they were working in the patch,
He walked unto the humble bed
And lifted up the snow-white spread;
A moment gazed around him there,
Then left a package tied with care.
Next time the farmer passed that way
Was on the pleasant picnic day,

And Maggie met him at the place
With her new dress and smiling face;
Placed there her midget hand in his,
Put up her mouth to get a kiss;
Upon him bent her eyes so blue,
Because he seemed he nothing knew,
And whispered to him, light as dew,
"I know 'twas you, I know 'twas you."

THE KEY OF THE BASTILE.

[General La Fayette, in 1789, presented to General Washington the key of the celebrated prison, the Bastile. The key is fastened to the wall in the state parlor at Mount Vernon.]

THE PRISON.

FIVE hundred years have passed away
Since your proud turrets, grim and gray,*
Were lifted up in darkest hour
To signalize a tyrant's power
Thy walls alone, immense and strong,
Have been the theme of many a song;
And many a sad and mournful tale
Has caused the stoutest heart to quail,
To mention which the cheek grows pale,
Of noble men and princes, too,
Who sudden passed from earthly view,
And languished in thy dungeons vile,
Bereft of joy and friendly smile,
Till naught was left to tell their thrall
Except the record on the wall,

---

* The Bastile was built in 1369. It had eight huge round towers, connected by curtains of masonry.

Which told the time when earth and sky
Were shut from them for aye and aye.

THE PRISONERS.

And never will there be a pen
Can give thy horrors unto men,
Or brush to make the canvas show
The speechless wretchedness and woe
Of hundreds who were thrust within
Thy walls of filth, and death, and sin;
Who never heard a gentle word,
Or listened to a warbling bird;
Who never heard a child's sweet laugh,
Nor did they freedom's waters quaff,
Nor ever had a reason given*
Why they were shut from light and heaven;
But hidden in thy den of pride
They, lone and wasted, pined and died.

THE SECRETS.

No! Never will thy secrets dread
Among the sons of men be spread;
For some of royal state were there
Who perished in their wild despair,
And never was the secret torn
From those who kept them, for they'd sworn
That never should a word be spoke
To those whose lives and hearts they broke;
And none who undertook the task
Did e'er reveal the Iron Mask.†

THE STORMING OF THE PRISON.

But Freedom's banner was unfurled

---

* The "lettre de cachet" was never explained.
† The Iron Mask is a secret to this day.

To float in glory 'round the world,
That every land, from sea to sea,
Might catch the song of liberty;
And, burning in the sons of France,
They turned their fiery, flaming glance
Upon the stern and hated thing
Whose walls kept secrets for the King,
And in their mighty strength they tore
From off its hinges the great door;
And there, before the sun was set,
With shout of joy and loud acclaim,
Beneath the eye of La Fayette,
They stormed the place in Freedom's name,
Set every helpless prisoner free,
And to La Fayette gave the key,
Who, when the brilliant work was done,
Brought it to our own Washington.

MOUNT VERNON.

Where could a spot of earth be found,
If you should search the world around,
A place more fit to keep in view
That sign of what fierce tyrants do,
Than that where brave Columbia's son,
The loved, immortal Washington,
Sleeps by Potomac's rolling tide—
A nation's boast, a nation's pride?
Himself a son of Freedom true,
Who dared to do, and well did do;
Who gave, this side the mighty deep,
A boon for us to always keep—
The boon of peace, and joy, and rest,
Where all the helpless may be blest;
And where, we trust, in all the years to come,
Freedom shall find her sweet and happy home.

BROTHER.

Lines on receiving the following letter on my 52d birthday.

WASHINGTON, April 24, 1880.

HON. R. B. VANCE, 223 E Street, Washington, D. C.—*My Dearest Brother:* Please regard the accompanying present as a small evidence of the love and ever-increasing affection of your only brother. You are fifty-two years old to-day; I will be fifty on the 13th of May. If there has ever been a shadow between us, I do not know it. God grant that the brotherly sunshine may continue until the end. God bless you and all that you love. Your brother,

Z. B. VANCE.

THANKS, brother, thanks!　Each tender, loving word
Hath in my soul a full remembrance stirred
Of things in life which have to us occurred.

I call to mind the spot where we were born,
The apple-trees, the fields of standing corn,
The mountain peaks bathed in the glowing morn;

The quiet graveyard on the big, red hill
Above the meadow, and the old corn-mill
Where the majestic oak is standing still.

And yonder, too, I once again can see
Where, while we sported in our boyish glee,
I got a fall from the persimmon-tree.*

And doubtless you, like me, remember well
The dear old church adown the pleasant dell,
Which nor tall steeple had, nor sounding bell

To call the people there to worship God—
To live in fear before his awful rod,
That they might sleep in peace when 'neath the sod.

---

* True to the old legend—a Carolinian loves persimmons.

Yes, we remember well that sunny day
When the good old man's* hands upon us lay,
Who from his face the tears did wipe away,

As gentle mother, and dear father, too,
Brought us to the congregation's glad view,†
To show us there the way, so good and true.

And now there comes a most delicious dream
Of years gone by which o'er our spirits gleam,
Upon the rushing Tahkeeostee stream.‡

There is the bathing in the wild river,
To think of which doth make the bosom quiver,
As on the bright, clear waters rushed forever.

And memory takes us to that river's side
Where by a little grave the waters glide,
We think of him—the lovely boy who died.

And every peak which rose all rugged there,
And gleamed in brightness in God's upper air,
Hath kissed our flying feet, so red and bare.

But, O my brother, where's the tongue can tell
The joy and grief which in our bosoms swell,
As on these things the miser heart doth dwell?

Long since in peace our father slept with God,
And darling mother, with God's staff and rod,¶
Is laid away beneath the churchyard sod.

My brother dear, you say, "Unto the end,"
Which Heaven in mercy to us ever send,
That here we may be truly brother—friend.

---

* Rev. Mr. Porter.   † In the beautiful baptismal rite.
‡ French Broad.   ¶ Psalm xxiii. 4.

6

But, brother, is this world "the end," indeed,
And earthly good in truth the noblest meed?
Or does the glory yet to come exceed *

The earthly in splendor as yet untold,
As silver is outshone by the bright gold,
'Or beds of quartz by diamonds they may hold?

And shall we not, beyond this vale of tears,
Meet all who shared our joys, our hopes, our fears,
And dwell with them through all the endless years?

God be our trust, our way, our truth, our friend,
That on his arm we ever may depend,
And heaven at last the peaceful, happy "end."

LOVE YOUR ENEMIES.

A True Story of the First Revolution.†

It was eve. The full-orb'd sun was setting
 In the far-off west; the mountain and plain
Were bath'd in gold, in the soul begetting
 Joys so keen that they almost seem'd as pain;
But, though the earth was lovely, and the sky
 Serene in its unchangeable glory,
The red fight all day had raged 'mid the cry
 And death-shout of foemen grim and gory.

                              'Twas then,
 As the shock of battle was drifting slow
To its final calm, two desperate men
 With matted hair and vengeful eyes, aglow
Like the tiger's fire in each, closed in strife

---

* Romans viii. 18.
† The substance of this piece the author saw in "a tale" some years ago.

The deadliest man may know; hand to hand,
Nor gun, nor blade impending; the dark knife
  Alone was unsheathed and clutch'd—proper brand
For those whose hate was mortal. Both were brave,
  And one was Whig, and one with Tory blood
Disgrac'd; and there the unsatisfied grave
  Open'd its mouth, where true and false they stood.

              The struggle's o'er,
  And the dripping knife is descending quick
For the felon foe; and the angry shore
  Of the eternal world, a vision thick
With awe to traitor hearts, before him came.
  What stays the blow? The patriot strikes not;
But, while his heart is fire, his eye is flame,
  He bears his foe from that sequestered spot
Calmly, till upon the furthermost verge
  Of a startling gorge and precipice deep
He halts to throw him thence, that there his dirge
  May be the roar of the river's wild leap.

         "Mercy! O mercy, now!"
  The Tory's voice was husk as thus he pray'd;
And dark red spots were on his cheek and brow
  As the strong man still held him there, and played
With his fears. "Where's my brother whom ye slew?
  Did you have mercy when with hollow voice,
For sake of wife and babes, the ones which grew
  By him, he pleaded they might still rejoice?"
He spake, "I could not save him." "Thou liest!
And, by Him who rules above, thou diest!"

                Again,
With lifted hands and agonizing fear,
  Where yet was seen, in all its darksome stain,
The work of blood, he begg'd he might appear

Before the widow'd one of him he'd slain.
Then, smiling grim, the patriot bound him fast,
   And through the forest dense and green wildwood,
Till sylvan scenes of varied hue were past,
   Led him where the orphans spent their childhood.

          'Twas a lonely home,
  Within a mountain vale and hidden dell,
Where rare, if e'er, the great of earth may come;
   But still a gentle place, casting a spell
Of witchery o'er the heart as you gaze
   Upon the trailing vine which climbs the door,
And in its fragrant boughs at once displays
   A cultur'd hand, though true that hand is poor.

       Not many years had come and gone,
  With light and shade to mark the mourner's face;
As in her home she sat and look'd upon
   The men that came, and in one glance did trace
The murderer's guilt.   Beside her stood her girl
   In childish grace, and near her stalwart boy;
One with proud step, and one with many a curl
   On her sweet head; and both a mother's joy.
The open book of God before her lay;
   And, in the quiet eve and twilight still,
Her broken heart in faithful vow did say
   That He alone should guide her by His will.

       He came; the murd'rer came,
And, with wild cry and low, despairing tone,
   Embrac'd her knees, and call'd her honor'd name;
Begged piteously for life, and did own
   His guilt—the stroke which well his arm did aim.
For a moment her brow was stern; the rush
   Of blood to cheek and eye was fierce and free,

And then it was calm, in the heart's deep hush,
  As she said, "God shall judge 'twixt thee and me.
My boy shall ope this book, his finger rest
  Upon a verse, and it shall speak of death
And life." Now see them there: the heaving breast
  Of the guilty one, and the half-drawn breath
Of the strong, excited brother; the child,
  As with flushed brow he stands 'tween death and life,
And lays his hand that none had e'er beguiled
  On the bless'd book which bids men cease their strife.
'Twas quickly done; the tender hand hath lit;
  And now the boy's is on the mother's eye
As, bending down, she sees the word is writ:
  "The man that did this thing shall surely die."*
A cry was heard; the wretch was closely hemmed;
  The dreadful knife no longer life will give.
"See! see! e'en God's thy guilty soul condemn'd.
  Prepare to die! Thou canst not, shalt not live!"

          One effort more he claimed:
  Let little Mary's finger try for him
The sacred word; and if again it named
  For death he'd go, though sure the vale was dim.
She came—the angel child—so sweet and bright,
  It seem'd a cherub from the upper skies
Had pass'd on wings of peace, with a strange light
  Adorning her wee face and tiny eyes.
Her hand was laid upon her mother's head,
  Then lifted up, as though her God to please;
Then sought the verse, which low the mother read:
  "I say unto you, Love your enemies."†
The spell was gone; the voice of mercy spoke
  To each bosom; the dying Jesus smil'd

---

* David and Nathan.   † Jesus.

On their torn hearts; each chord they silent broke,
  And loos'd him in the forest lone and wild.

'Twas night; the battle's stern and dread array
  Was o'er; stillness held the pulse of the world,
And many who in life had spent the day
  Were stark and cold, their shrouds around them furl'd.
Within that cot, now desolate and sad
  For want of his (the father's, husband's) smile,
They all were gronp'd.   If he who made them glad
  Could come, they thought, for just a little while
And speak, though in dead garb his soul were clad,
  They'd feel e'en yet this earth some pleasures had.
Hark! was't the wind which stirr'd the stilly night,
  Or wild cat's leap, or panther's stealthy tread?
What form is that which darkens now the light?
  O God! 'tis he whom long we thought was dead!
The wife!—she starts, then laughs, then sudden weeps,
  And scarce believes, though kind embrace is giv'n;
While 'round his breast each baby sweetly creeps,
  And the lone cot seems now another heav'n.

His tale was gladly told.   The Tory's blade
  Had pierc'd his breast, but not a mortal blow
Inflicted; then true friends the blood had staid,
  And thence he'd come to turn to joy their woe.
And now the father oped the book of God
  And joyfully read, his clear voice ringing,
" He chast'neth whom He loveth with His rod;"
  And, pausing, he led the sacred singing:
        How sweet to know that Jesus' arm
          Is 'round us evermore;
        To feel we are secure from harm,
          Though lone, and weak, and poor;

To see each day his mercy nigh,
  Protection for each head;
And hear him in the wind's low sigh,
  Or in the thunder dread.
Dear Savior, let thy blesséd love
  Fill all our hearts with peace,
And in thy counsels let us move
  Till life itself shall cease;
Then, fondly rising in thy name,
  When life and earth are past,
Go back to thee, from whom we came,
  All safe in heav'n at last.

'Twas then the voice of prayer was heard: how sweet
  It rises on the wings of peace, an incense
Holy to Him above; and who doth greet
  The yearning soul, its covert and defense.
And she, who'd sorrow'd with most touching grief,
  Who for the dead had mourn'd with widow'd weeds,
Look'd forth upon the wondrous night with brief
  Glance at the starry worlds—fiery steeds
Of light, which move in their eternal round.
  The far-off gems were sparkling in their orbs,
And ev'ry star did seem as if 'twas crown'd
  With jewels; but that which most her soul absorbs,
And stirs it to its very depths profound,
As though 'twas written there to heal each wound,
  Was this: "The dead's alive! the lost is found!"

LINES

On Receiving a Box of Edibles for the Mess, at Fort Delaware.

WHEN first this world was brought to light
  The Lord made Father Adam,

But not until all things were right
   Did He bring out the Madam.
It was at first, without a doubt,
   Our Maker's kind decision
To see if Adam could make out
   Without that rib incision.

In order, then, to try the plan,
   And prove it not a hard one,
The angels brought the new-made man
   And placed him in the garden;
Then pointed out the animals,
   And talk'd about the weather,
And not to fear the cannibals,
   But keep his stock together.

Now, when the beasts went after hay,
   Adam began to name them,
Which made the monkeys romp and play—
   And who, indeed, could blame them?
And this a while did occupy
   His time and good intentions;
But still his mind, I can't tell why,
   Would think of new inventions.

And then he walked among the flowers,
   And pull'd the pinks and roses;
And saunter'd in the shady bowers,
   The place for rests and dozes.
But 'twas no use; his soul was sad;
   All things about did shock it;
He sigh'd around, though strangely clad,
   With hands in breeches pocket.

Then the dear Lord put him to sleep,
   With orders not to wake him

Till Eve should from the lilies creep
    With sly intent to take him.
And when he wak'd, the happy dog,
    He rubb'd his eyes a new man;
Unless some thing his sight did clog,
    There sat a pretty woman.

And ever since, in time of need,
    The darlings do attend us;
And when our hearts with ills do bleed,
    They're ready to befriend us.
And even when we're scarce of "tack,"
    And they should chance to hear it,
They send us boxes full of "snack,"
    And tell "the mess" to share it.

I'M THINKING OF THEE NOW, MY DEAR.

I'M thinking of thee now, my dear,
    Behind these bars and prison walls,
And list'ning to the music clear
    Of thy lov'd voice, as oft it calls;
And then I see before mine eye
    Thy form and both our children, too,
And fancy shows me Jimmie try
    The tricks which seemed forever new.

There's not a day, and not an hour,
    Which passeth o'er this weary heart,
But there's a meeting in thy bower
    In which we all do have a part.
'Tis now we're in the garden walks,
    Anon beneath the cedar-trees,

Then hand in hand we gave our talks
   Among the flowers that kiss the breeze.

And thy dear head is on my breast,
   As fond, as lovingly as when
I took thee from the parent nest—
   Thy home up in the mountain glen.
And then we sit upon the lawn,
   With both the babies at our feet,
While golden hours are passing on,
   To all our hearts surpassing sweet.

And often, on the lone, gray hill,
   We wander to the churchyard, where
Our other children lie so still
   Beneath the grass that's growing there;
And once again each little eye
   Grows tender for the wonted kiss,
And, though our hearts are breaking nigh,
   We feel they nothing know but bliss.

And oft in sleep, my darling one,
   While 'round me rears the fort's grim wall,
Before the night's dark watch is done,
   I dream of thee, and home, and all;
And sure I feel it is thy arm
   Around my neck with warm caress,
And in that holy, happy charm
   Forget the chains which on me press.

Many a fair and lovely form
   Hath crossed my path and bless'd my way;
Many a heart and bosom warm
   Hath cheer'd me since my captive day;

But 'mong them all, though good they be,
　And well adorn pure virtue's throne,
Not one can ever be to me
　What thou hast been, my love, my own.

Fort Delaware, 1864.

LINES

On Receiving a Pillow at Fort Delaware.

THOU lady, kind, if thanks impart
　A glow of pleasure to the brow,
And bringeth gladness to the heart,
　Let me unto thee give them now;
For sure I feel thy timely gift
　Hath manifested friendship true,
Which makes my bosom the more swift
　To bless thee, and the pillow, too.

Each night my head lay on my boots,
　Which total baldness e'er portends;
And well I know this illy suits
　The lovely ones I call my friends.
But now 'tis gone, the danger's o'er,
　My pillowed dreams are of the fair;
And now I feel forevermore
　I'll love them all, and save my hair.

LINES

Sent to Miss LIZZIE W., Chestertown, Maryland.

'TWAS evening, and in the far-off west
　The clouds were gorgeous with the lovely hues

Of a strange beauty; the homes of the blest,
   Whose flowers are moisten'd with celestial dews,
May well be like it; and the calm, deep bay
   Did seem as if it was a thing of life;
Evincing life, though, only as its spray
   Did lave the shore in frolic more than strife.
There was one—a captive—who sadly gazed
   Upon the water, the ships, and the shore;
The fields where children play'd and cattle graz'd;
   And God's free air is felt, which e'en the poor
May enjoy; and his heart did yearn to break
   His prison bars, and seek the woodland wild,
The song of birds, the hum of bees, and take
   One look at earth, as though he were a child
Once more; and then the Sabbath's quiet voice
   Spoke in soothing tones to his weary breast,
Bidding him e'en in trouble to rejoice,
   And know the faithful yet shall find a rest.
And then the scene was chang'd: the captive slept;
   Before his dreaming eye a gentle home
Appear'd; the jessamines and roses kept
   Watch at the door, and whisper'd ever, " Come! "
And words of love were kindly spoken there
   By forms that mov'd about the house, the lawn,
And yard.   Ah, 'twas a peaceful scene, and fair,
   Such as makes new joys 'pon the heart to dawn.
The elder, in the pleasant eve of age,
   A matron good, they sweetly hail'd as " Mother,"
And e'en the bird which nestled in its cage
   The others as sisters knew.   One—a brother—
Was missing, and well they knew the wild rage
Of battle might reach him; and sad presage
Was mix'd with hope, which did their fears assuage.

                                   Blessed seat
Of innocence and pleasure! may no hand
    Break rudely on thy sunny walks and sweet
Society; though war devastate the land,
    And thousands—friends and foes—fall in the heat
Of the red fight, by saber, gun, or brand,
    May they who grace thy halls lead lives of joy,
    And gain, at last, a rest without alloy.

Fort Delaware, 1864.

A MOTHER TO HER BABE.

SHE was young, pure, and strangely beautiful;
    Her golden hair, with many a soft curl,
So full of witch'ry in the dutiful
    And good of earth, as though she were a girl
Even yet, hung 'round her snowy neck, fit
    Companion for the lustrous, speaking eye,
The damask cheek, where blushes come and flit
    E'en as a bird which 'mong the boughs doth fly.
Her brow was high and noble, the bright stamp
    Of a Master Workman, the living trace
Of a glorious Architect; time's tramp
    Had lightly touch'd each true and winning grace,
    But still enough to mold the charming face.

And joy was there: upon her happy breast,
    The home of innocence and holy love,
A sweet wee thing, a birdlet in its nest,
    With cherub form, the gift of Him above,
Ope'd its tiny eyes and smiled; then his hand
    Did pull the sunny curls which fell around
His little head, peeping through at the bland,
    Mild face bent o'er him, till the profound

Depths of her mother heart with gushing bliss
O'erflowed, and lip met lip in one long kiss.
    O, a mother's love! thanks be unto God!
Though the world is selfish, and hard, and stern,
    And o'er our hearts the unpitying rod
Of tyranny may sweep, one heart will yearn
    And beat for us till laid beneath the sod.

The baby slept; and his silken lashes
    Clos'd gently o'er the blue and tender eyes,
Those eyes from which such a rapt light flashes
    As makes us feel 'tis less of earth than skies;
And as he slept upon that bosom fair,
    Pillow'd so cozy in his mother's arms,
He smile·l again, as if while sleeping there
    An angel bless'd him with its pretty charms.
Then, bending low, my face was brought so near
    To his that I caught the rustle which springs
From fairy forms and falls upon the ear
    As music, or the rush of silver wings
In the stilly air; and through that still air,
    Like a spirit lute, melodiously strung,
A voice was heard, so eloquent, so rare,
    That fancy said, It is a seraph's tongue:
        Sleep, little baby, sleep!
            Thou'rt safe on that true arm;
        An unseen hand doth keep
            Thee free from earthly harm;
        Thy mother's care,
        And earnest prayer,
            Shall hide thee still from all alarm.
        Sleep, little baby, sleep!
            For stronger arms than hers

Guard thee with care so deep,
　　So intent, that it stirs
The tender mind
And bosom kind
　　Of Him whose mercy never errs.

SONG—NEVER TAKE THE OATH.

AIR: *Hey Tuttie Tattie, or Bruce's Address.*

[At Camp Chase, Ohio, and Fort Delaware it was quite common for persons—meaning well, no doubt—to come into the prison and invite the Southern soldiers to take the oath and be released. Hence the song.]

SOLDIER, friend, and brother, too,
While our flag of "bonny blue"—
Emblem of the brave and true—
　　Kisses still the gale,
Gather up your manhood's might.
What! though gloomy be the night,
'Tis not Northmen can affright—
　　Heroes never quail!

Let their oath fall to the ground;
Pass their offers all around;
Nobler boons than theirs are found:
　　Liberty's own call.
Voices now are in the air,
'Bove us, 'round us, ev'rywhere,
Whispering of our country fair,
　　Lov'd ones, home, and all.

Soldier, listen! do not start!
Freedom's speaking to each heart:
" Firmly, sternly act your part

Till the strife is o'er!"
Shall her voice to you be vain?
Shall our fields of trampled grain,
    Bones of friends which bleach the plain,
        Stir you up no more?

See! the Yankee cohort comes!
See! our charr'd and ruin'd homes!
See! around our churches' domes
        Flames are mounting high!
God of justice, truth, and right,
Rouse the soldier for the fight!
Let the fires of freedom light
        When to do or die!

Fort Delaware, 1864.

NOEL.

THOU art gone, my brother!   No more
This side the everlasting shore
Shall lip and brow between us meet
In fond embrace and welcome sweet.

Thou art gone, dear brother!   The hill
Above our home is rugged still,
And the tall rock, with jagged head,
Keeps watch around thy narrow bed.

Thou art gone, my brother!   The flower
That lur'd thee in that fatal hour
Each year doth bloom with fragrant smell
Upon the cliff* from whence thou fell.

-----

* In 1840, or thereabouts, he was trying to get a flower on the edge of a precipice, lost his foothold, fell, and received a wound from which he never recovered.

Thou art gone, my brother! The rush
Of the river,* with its swift gush
Of waters, charms the listening ear,
But thine no more, my brother dear.

Thou art gone, dear brother! The place
Where once was seen thy pleasant face
Is lone and wasted; e'en the yard
By war's rude tramp is sadly marr'd.

Thou art gone, dear brother! Thy dirge
Upon the river's foaming verge
Is the waves' lullaby, soft, low,
As if the waters, too, felt woe.

Yes, dearest brother, thou art gone,
And though the march of time is on,
Thy noble brow and clear blue eye
Are beaming now where none can die.

ACROSTIC.

["Aunt Lizzie" is a very poor old lady in ——, who toils with her needle for the Confederate soldiers at Point Lookout and Fort Delaware, devoting more than half of her earnings to those unfortunate prisoners of war.]

ALL hail to virtue, in its pure and priceless worth!
Unknown, perchance, and humble from its very birth;
Not kings and princes, with their grand and gaudy toys,
The sweeter ends of life attain without its joys.

---

* French Broad at Marshall, N. C.

7

Each day, fore'er, this gift of God more brightly glows,
Like rainbow hues when clouds are gone and tempests
　　close.
In time it schools the soul and lays pure treasures up,
Zealous for others' good, a draught which angels sup;
And though it toils in poverty's most lowly vale,
By the side of frail forms, whose brows and cheeks are
　　pale,
Enchanting riches clothe it with the happy power
To live again beyond death's painful, trying hour,
Heaven being its home, the fields on high its bower.

　　Fort Delaware, 1864.

THE DYING SOLDIER—A TRUE INCIDENT.

[A Confederate prisoner of war at Camp Chase, Ohio, was lying
on his bunk in a dying state. His brother soldiers kept vigil at
his side. At length he was quite still, and all thought the struggle
over, when he suddenly rallied, opened his eyes, and said, "Boys,
never take the oath: the country is safe, the Confederacy will be
triumphant," and expired at once.]

THE wintry wind went howling by with drear and pierc-
　　ing breath,
As on his couch a soldier lay, the victim of grim death;
For on him then the icy hand was closing hard and fast,
His dying sighs commingling sad with evening's solemn
　　blast.

Not one was there of all he'd known, in better times than
　　these,
To smooth his brow, to kiss his cheek, or give his bosom
　　ease;
For far from them the stricken one was failing slow and
　　sure,

Nor precious pets nor tender friends were there to weep
or cure.

His home was in the bonny South, the land of sun and
flowers,
And far away the household band did pass the weary
hours;
And night and morn they offered up, within his distant
home,
The prayer that God would bring him thence, but still he
did not come.

And e'en his babes would query oft of their fond mother
true,
"Why don't dear papa come again to meet with us and
you?"
And broken hearts and tears were there to mark the
absent one,
Who linger'd in his foeman's grasp, life's conflict nearly
done.

But not with anguish on his sight this touching vision
fell;
His God, he knew, was kind and just, "He doeth all
things well;"
From Him they came, to Him he gave. Then, with a
chasten'd will,
He sank upon his lowly bed, till life itself seem'd still.

We watch'd him as he calmly lay, and thought that all
was o'er:
His martial step and manly voice we'd see and hear no
more;
Nor in the battle's fierce array would he for country stand;
His pure, heroic soul had fled into the dreamless land!

But, strange to tell, he mov'd again, and ope'd his dying
    eye,
While on his face a smile was seen of purpose noble, high;
"All's right," he said; "reject the oath; my native South
    will win!"
And then his soldier spirit pass'd away from earth and sin.

A strange, wild thrill ran through us all as these brave
    words were said,
And many a stern, undaunted eye the tear of sorrow shed;
And vows were spoke from mouth to mouth by ev'ry
    Southland son,
"May God to us do so and more if e'er this thing is done!"

THE TWO KNIGHTS.

[Look on this Picture.]

FULL knightly, 'mid the clashing
    Of shining sword and lance,
Where charged the mailéd squadrons
    Upon the foe's advance,
Sir Jethrel held in hand
The banner of his band
    O'er the red field's expanse.

Around him were the dying
    In their ghastly array,
And far away the shouting
    Was heard along the way,
Where men incased in steel
Made there their foemen feel
    The sternness of the fray.

The battle raged with fury
  Throughout the serried host,
As breaks the mighty billows
  Upon the rocky coast;
And gallant knight and steed
Upon that field did bleed
  Where might was needed most.

Sometimes the fiery squadrons
  Break through the f e's align,
And shout with martial rapture
  Where plumes and helmets shine;
But once again the foe
Recovers from the blow,
  And forms anew his line.

Sir Jethrel led his legions
  With glave, and dirk, and spear,
In the very teeth of battle,
  Nor felt a twinge of fear;
But as his foaming steed
Bore him to gallant deed,
  A lance-head pierced his gear.*

Down in the dread encounter,
  Upon the blood-red field,
With stained and broken armor,
  He rested on his shield;
Nor shall he rise again
From off that bloody plain,
  Though every foe should yield.

And as the evening shadows
  Are gathering 'round his head,

---

* Military harness.—*Jamieson.*

He strains his ear to listen
  For word from those who bled;
But all around was still,
Save a bugle on the hill,
  For other sounds were dead,

Except the mournful moaning
  Of some poor wounded one
Who's fought his fatal battle
  ·Before that setting sun;
And, by his comrade true,
Beneath the falling dew,
  His sands of life have run.

The dying knight was dreaming
  Of the· land he loved so well,·
And a fair and stainless maiden
  Whose love had cast a spell
Around his manly heart
Before he did depart
  To the field whereon he fell.

But, though his fame was brilliant,
  And mighty was his arm,
As, dying in his glory,
  He felt a soldier's charm;
Yet in his dying face
One could but see the trace
  Of blood, and death, and harm;

For only fierce ambition
  Had led him to the field,
For the rapture of the conflict
  As in *its* might it pealed;
And nothing *now* was left

For that soul of peace bereft
  But to die upon his shield.

[Now Look on This.]

Along a rugged pathway,
  Upon the mountain side,
A knight toiled up the ascent
  To reach the mountain's pride;
For just beyond the peak,
In a valley on the creek,
  Lay the spot to which he hied.

His form was tall and manly,
  And in his eagle eye
Was seen the lofty courage
  To fight his fight or die;
And, armed from head to heel
In stronger mail than steel,
  He was clad for daring high.

His helmet of salvation
  Gleamed in the mountain air,
And on his stalwart bosom
  The shield of faith shone fair;
And in his willing hand,
On that lone mountain strand,
  His blade of truth was bare.

The breastplate of the righteous
  Was o'er his faithful breast,
And the gospel preparation
  'Round his feet was firmly pressed;
Yea, his feet were truly shod
With the peace which comes from God,
  As on he went with zest.

As the soldier mounted higher
  Along the mountain road,
And nature in her gladness
  Around him peaceful glowed,
His song of bounding joy,
Without the least alloy,
  O'er all the forest flowed.

Salvation was the burden—
  Salvation for the world—
Of his grand and holy music
  As the clouds about him whirled;
And the music in the air
Was of conquest brave and fair,
  For it all the earth impearled.

When the soldier reached the station,
  He found the people there,
And a song of exultation
  Was floating on the air:
"The Lord my shepherd is;*
He gives me peace and bliss,"
  They sang, and knelt in prayer.

The soldier used his weapon—
  A blade of temper keen—
With skill in every motion
  As it cut the joints between;†
For it proved its metal pure;
The thrust that killed did cure,
  And the dead alive were seen!

Thus in the mighty battle
  The soldier fought for God,

---

* Psalm xxiii.   † Hebrews iv. 12.

And waved the gospel banner
  O'er the hills on which he trod,
Till death on his pale horse
Left the soldier's manly corse
  To rest beneath the sod.

Not in the battle's thunder,
  Where cannon flamed with fire;
Not where the rushing squadrons
  Might glut their fiercest ire,
Did the soldier pass to rest
With hands upon his breast,
  ·As if his feet did tire;

But 'mid the angels shining,
  As round their squadron swings,
The soldiers tall of heaven
  Upheld him with their wings;
And, forever borne away
To the fields of endless day,
  God's soldier rests and sings.

TO REV. I. W. K. HANDY, D.D., POLITICAL PRISONER.

THERE is a secret tie between
  Our hearts for reasons more than one,
Which winter's cold nor summer's sheen
  Can wear away and say begone;
I feel it oft in solitude,
  As well as when the crowd is nigh,
And sure it gives my spirit food
  To battle on till life is by.

Yea, often when thy voice is heard
 In earnest plea that all may turn,
Methinks I gather from each word
 A love which makes my bosom burn;
For well I know thy inmost thought
 Is that we all may live and do
Those things with peaceful blessings fraught
 When earth is gone and heav'n in view.

The weary months have flown since first
 We met within these prison walls,
Not pleasant days like those of erst
 When quiet in our own dear halls;
But never, though the iron hand
 Press'd rudely on thy patriot breast,
Could aught but patient will be scann'd
 To His wise rule who knoweth best.

And many here will bless thy name,
 Their teacher in the path of good,
Since in their hearts the Spirit's flame
 Hath lit up such a happy mood;
For well I ween it was thy care,
 Directed by the Spirit's glow,
Which led them to the Savior, where
 All alike may mercy know.

And now thy footsteps soon shall tend
 To that dear land we love so well,
And brighter prospects soon shall blend
 Beneath the charm of Southland's spell.
Dear Doctor, go; I give thee up,
 With prayer that God will keep thee free;

And only ask, when that sweet cup
Shall overflow, to pray for me.

Most fraternally yours, R. B. V.

Fort Delaware, 1864.

THE CAPTIVE ELEPHANT.

Sometimes the newly captured animal lies down, refuses to move
or to take food, and in a very short time dies, without the agency
of any known or perceptible disease. The natives call it "dying
of a broken heart."—*A Peep at the Elephant.*

POOR beast! I deeply sympathize with thy
Great sorrow, and wonder not that in a
Case so mournful as thine the wheels of life
Should cease to move, and e'en thy giant heart,
Depriv'd of God's best gift to thee, poor brute,
Should break its chords, its mighty strength. No
    more
In the jungle wild, nor on the plain, nor
In the mysterious valley, the haunts
And homes of thy kindred, the very scenes
Where thou didst rear thy young, and train them
    there,
Shall thy huge form display its dreadful front.
Alas! alas! the tyrant holds thee fast!
His chains shall rivet close thy pond'rous feet,
And the shackles of a feeble race shall
Hold thee in "durance vile," an abject slave
To his own will, his own low lust of gain.
  Thou'rt not alone, poor beast, in suffering.
'Tis written well by one who felt and knew
That "Man's inhumanity to man makes
Countless thousands mourn;" and 'tis even so.

The desolated field and burning home,
The fatherless child and helpless widow,
The wasted heritage and ruin'd maid,
And tears, and blood, and death—the black shadow
Of a nameless woe—all, all proclaim 'tis true.
　　O, Liberty! how sweet thou art!
When even the untutored beast doth mourn
Thy absence, and in his speechless sorrow
Lay him down before his time to die!
　　Beautiful and blesséd spirit! thou cam'st
From heaven, and on thy hallowed wings
The smile of God is shining, and thy brow
Is radiant with a deathless light.   Let
Me learn of thee a lesson pure, and do
Unto all men as they should do to me.

Fort Delaware, 1864.

GOOD NEWS FROM HOME.

Good news from home by mail last night!
　　My wife and babies all are well;
This morn my heart is free and bright
　　With feelings more than I can tell.
Thank God!   He gives me comfort yet,
　　Unworthy, though, and sinful, too;
Then O, my spirit, cease to fret
　　About the things ye can't undo!

Be strong, my soul! trust thou in God!
　　These clouds, though dark and gloomy now,
May pass thee 'neath His chast'ning rod,
　　And burst with mercies o'er my brow.

Who knows it all?   Each darken'd edge
  May soon be tinged with silver hue:
Will not the King redeem His pledge
  To all who try to serve Him true?

'Tis e'er with us, as with the day,
  The brightest ones do but portend
That sunshine clear must pass away,
  And clouds and storms be in the end;
But when they come, we soon shall see
  A rift not made with human hands,
And far away a light shall be
  To guide us to the heav'nly lands.

THE GRAPE-VINE LINE.

PROFESSOR MORSE
  Thought him a horse
When first he put in motion
  His 'graphic wires,
  And lightning flyers,
From mountain down to ocean;
  And ev'ry one
  Thought he had done
The grandest thing in nature.
  But let him come
  To "Johnny's" * home,
And see a stranger "crayture."

  'Tis on this isle †
  He'll grin and smile,
And ope his eyes with wonder,

---

* Name given Southern soldiers by the Federals.
† Fort Delaware is built upon " Pea Patch " Island, in Delaware River.

When he shall hear
From far and near
The grape-vine speak its thunder.
Sometimes 'tis heard
By flying word
From t'other side of Jordan,*
And each dispatch,
Though hard to catch,
Contains some things unheard on.
And then again,
Through mud and rain,
It kites around the "bull-pen;" †
And ev'ry eye
Grows brighter by
The line that so doth gull men.
But if you want
To hear us rant,
When each his jargon utters,
Put on your shoes,
What else you choose,
And go out to the sutler's.
Here we arrange
For our exchange—
Our speedy separation;
And when we're back
We'll not be slack
To whip the Yankee nation.

Long wave the grape!
And let us gape;

---

* The "barracks," where Southern private soldiers were confined.

† The open space, or campus, between the officers' and privates' barracks.

It's rousing, lively, funny;
Though surely it
Each one hath hit,
'Tis good for " Rebby Johnny."

SACRED VIBRATIONS.

" Let there be light." (Genesis i. 3.)

" In the beginning" all things slept;
The uncreated years and still ages
Of a dreamless era, where silence kept
Its lonely vigils, nor sprites nor sages
Did know its history, were shrouded all
In unbroken nonentity; the dark
Form of chaos, like a gigantic pall,
O'erhung the gloomy void; nor aught did mark
The coming of the mighty angel, Time,
Though grand his brow, and ev'ry step sublime.
On the waters, then,
The mysterious, ever restless flood,
A wondrous Spirit mov'd, the same to men
Unknown, but step and look proclaimed Him God.
With lifted arm, and wonder-working rod,
And awful voice, like thunders rolling by,
He spake the fiat dread, " Let there be light,"
And forth from the thick darkness o'er the sky,
The earth, the surging mass, the home of night
And bosom of the bill'wy deep, was seen
The magic of His will: before His sight
The hills appear'd, and the tall trees did nod
And wave their foliage o'er the smooth, green
Fields; and far away did star, and gem, and world

Move into being; while in the air, high
O'er all, the sun his banner bright unfurled;
   Joy was in heaven, and the melodious spheres
Caught the echo; while, through the distant isles
   And mystic chambers of eternity,
Sweet sounds, too sweet, alas! for mortal ears,
   Did charm the favor'd audience, the free
Spirits who bask in their Creator's smiles.
   Then, as worlds on worlds to their place did wheel
In the onward march of time, like the sound
   Of many waters as they swiftly steal
Upon the rock-bound coast, a voice profound
   Through suns, and hosts, and space did straight-
      way peal:
        Praise!   Praise!
        Him give all praise,
        "Ancient of days!"
      Praise, praise, praise! praise Him now!
      Him of the royal brow;
      The blesséd three in one,
      By whom this work was done;
      Sons of the morning, tall,
      Praise Him as God of all!
And you, ye happy throng,
Take up the joyous song!
Shout! shout! ye distant hills,
And streams, and floods, and rills!
Let ev'ry host and ev'ry gem
Catch up the strain from these and them,
Till all on earth and all in heaven
The meed of praise to Him hath given!

THE FADED VIOLETS

Received from a Young Lady in the South, while the Writer was a
Prisoner at Fort Delaware.

THEY were tiny and delicate: the wind
Might not touch them roughly with its drear breath,
For children of the sun, to cold unknown,
And of a sunny land, were they.   The hand
Of God did paint them there; with sweet perfume
Did fill each little cup, and make fragrant
The air of their nativity 'round them;
He alone did rear the flexible stem,
And cause the leaf to show its deep, deep green,
And then the bud to slowly ope its eye
To the light; and they came forth, soft and fair,
Strangers, as it were, in a cold, cold world.
    Yet not for nothing did they live: glad eyes
Have gaz'd upon them, and white hands have pluck'd
The noxious weed from near them; and many
Bright thoughts, perchance, have been about them had
By minds that are gentle; and they, doubtless,
Did give a softer hue even to these;
Lending e'en to woman's heart, lovely thing,
A glow, a joy, and a fadeless beauty.
    And thence, while fading, dying, they did come
To bless a dreamer in his prison cell,
And did speak him there, and say, whisp'ringly:

> " We are fading, we are fading,
>   Like early hopes away,
> And we soon shall lie forgotten
>   Beneath our mother clay;
> And nevermore upon the gale
>   Will we our perfume give:

8

'Tis said by God—who shall unsay?—
  ' Naught shall forever live.'

" We are fading, we are fading,
  Like clouds at break of morn,
Or as dieth on the mountain
  Sounds from the shepherd's horn;
Or even as the early dew
  Which falleth on the flowers,
And melts before the God of day,
  Hath told the morning hours.

" We are fading, we are fading,
  As all on earth must fade,
Till every thing that liveth
  The mournful debt hath paid.
Ah! even she who sent us here
  With kind and gentle hand,
And he to whom we now appear
  Will to the dreamless land.

" But when the spring-time comes once more
  O'er brook, and hill, and plain,
We from the precious parent stem
  Will spring to life again.
And so of you, and so of her—
  To all the hope is given—
The grave is no unbroken sleep,
  To keep ye from your heaven."

TO VIOLA.

I NEVER shall forget the place
  Where first I saw thee, maid divine;

Such sweetness cloth'd thy youthful face,
 So softly beamed those eyes of thine,
Each motion was so full of grace
 That this poor heart no more was mine.
Ah! little knew ye what ye did
 On that bright eve when first we met,
When Cupid soft unveil'd each lid,
 Strung fast his bow, his arrow set,
And sped the shaft that deeply hid
 Within my breast and pierceth yet,
Though days, and hours, and years have flown
Since first I sought thee for my own.

1848.

VIOLA AT THE FALLS.

I saw thee there with thy dark hair,
 And witching brow, and sparkling eye;
Thy form so rare, so queenly fair,
 That nature's beauties, growing by,
Did vainly stare, and seek to share
 The sweetness ling'ring in thy sigh.
What! though the cascade dash'd its foam
 On that proud cliff with gentle spray,
And nature revel'd in her home,
 'Mid flow'ry wilds, surpassing gay;
Not they had made my feet to roam,
 Not they had led my steps away;
'Twas thy dear self controll'd me still,
Thy voice that did this bosom thrill.

1848.

THE MOUNTAIN STORM.

DEDICATED TO CHRISTIAN REID.

[As one part of the design of the Historical Society is to pre-
serve poems written by North Carolinians, or about North Carolina,
we insert the following by one of North Carolina's honored sons,
and dedicated to one of her distinguished daughters. We would
be glad to receive and publish poems by natives of the State, especially such as have never been put in books.—*N. C. Journal of
Education.*]

I STÓOD upon a splintered peak
    Of my own Southland mountains,
And listened to the eagle's shriek
    Above the snow-white fountains;

And shouted till the echo rang
    O'er cliff, and crag, and valley,
Till the red deer from covert sprang
    Where swift-foot hunters rally.

O! lovely was the peaceful scene—
    The rock, the cascade hoary;
The forest with its shady sheen,
    The summer's crowning glory.

But noblest, 'mong its fellows proud,
    Of e'en the storm-fiend fearless,
The giant oak there kissed the cloud—
    A monarch grand and peerless.

But soon the wild winds swept the hills,
    Enshrouding them in madness,
And tore in shreds each thing that gilds
    The mountains in their gladness.

The modest flower, the mighty oak,
    Which fond the eye had cherish'd,

Were level'd by the fearful stroke,
　And both alike had perished.

No starry gem shed soft its light;.
　No moon gave forth its blessing;
No sunburst glinted mountain height,
　As if the world caressing;

No bird voice floated sweet along;
　No cloud rift showed the haven;
I only heard the tempest song,
　And croaking of the raven.

While round each peak, as if in wrath,
　Was heard the hurtling thunder;
And just behind the lightning's path
　The earth seemed burst asunder.

Ah me! I then cried out in fear,
　Will darkness ne'er be ended?
When, lo! around me, bright and clear,
　The rainbow's form was bended.

And graciously, on earth and sky,
　God's everlasting token
Proclaimed that, though the earth may die,
　His word shall ne'er be broken.

EPHPHATHA.

[Mark vii. 34.]

His feet were white with the dust of travel. Alone
He had come from Tyre and Sidon's heathenish coast,
And by Galilee's sea the sad stranger

Stayed his weary steps and taught. The people
Wondered who he was, and whence he came. Prophet
Indeed he seem'd, and gracious were his words,
As, with a face of gentle loveliness, he spake
As never man spake. From his matchless head
His long hair had fallen on his seamless coat,
And ne'er had human eye such beauty seen.
From far his fame had come, and memory
Stirred men's hearts by deeds that he had done
In Bethsaida and by fair Gennesaret's shore.
And now the evening tide was nigh; but still
He knew no rest, for on his heart men's woes
Oft pressed for kind relief and safe deliverance.
Not one of all who came had sued in vain:
E'en the woman who hungered for the crumbs
Which fell from the Master's bounteous table,
Not deeming it meet to give the bread to dogs,
In her humility and holy faith
There found the mild trav'ler a friend and brother.
Then they brought him one upon whose dull ear
No sound of joy had ever rested; earth
To him was soundless; no fond mother tones,
So soft, so low, so sweet, like zephyr sighs
'Mid beds of violets, filling the soul
With love unspeakable, had ever thrill'd him;
No child's laugh, almost all we've left of heaven—
So full of innocence—e'er charmed his soul;
No feather'd songster, in his leafy home,
For him had fill'd the woods with melody;
Ah! never had he breath'd a mother's name,
Nor called his child "my darling;" the strings of his
    tongue
Were tied and still, and sighs his only voice.

"They bring unto him," says the sacred word,
"The deaf," and mutely he stands before the seer,
While the Master's eyes are on him in love
And tenderest compassion. Mark the Lord!
No smile of proud disdain wreath'd His high mien;
No shrinking from the touch of wretchedness;
No sneer curl'd his lip at man's deformity;
But He who made and own'd unnumber'd worlds,
Grand in fatherhood, vast in riches, bowed
Sad and sorrowful beside the speechless one,
Leaving this a record: He loved the poor.
Long ago, God's prophet, stern and holy,
Look'd through the ages at the woman's seed,
And beheld Him there, "a man of sorrows
And with grief acquainted," and now He stood
With a world's griefs pressing His heart and soul.
Then, in the calm of eve, as the waters
Of the lake lay peaceful at His tired feet,
He led the deaf aside, and, looking up
To heaven's deep and endless fields of blue,
He sighed, and softly spoke, "Ephphatha."
O wondrous word! O thrilling sound! Gentle
As a mourner's sigh, light as thistle-down,
It pierced through cloud, and sky, and far-off star,
Till Heav'n did also hear; and the deaf ear
Its portals open'd at its Maker's voice,
Filling the stricken one with joy and awe.
Then in his gladness, as tremblingly he stood,
With tearful eye and swelling heart, gazing
On Mary's Son, the word he spoke, his first,
Was this, "Rabboni."

DR. MITCHELL'S GRAVE.

On the highest peak * of a mighty chain
   Of hill and mountain fastness,
Where nature doth her primal rule maintain
   Amid their solemn vastness,
There's a lonely grave that the mountains gave,
Which the sorrowing moonbeams gently lave.

No echoing sound of the city's hum
   Shall reach the peaceful sleeper;
No note of joy or grief to him shall come
   From plow-boy or from reaper;
But silent he'll sleep, while the ivies creep,
   And the angels their sacred vigils keep.

The deafening peals of the thunder's voice
   Shall never break his dreaming,
Though the tempests wild in their might rejoice
   Amid the lightning's gleaming;
His rest still is deep on the mountain steep,
Though his pupils mourn and his loved ones weep.

The tremulous trills of the mother bird,
   As she sings her songs so lowly,
Though a sweeter tone the ear never heard,
   Touch not a rest so holy;
For God keeps him there, in the upper air,
Sleeping and waiting for the morning fair.

The clustering blooms of the flowerets wild,
   Their fragrance sweet distilling,

---

* Seven thousand feet above tide-water—the highest peak of the
Appalachian chain.

Though ever himself kind nature's fond child,
   Break not the tryst he's filling;
For God knows so well the spot where he fell
That nothing but Heaven can unlock the spell.

The summer and autumn, they come and go,
   Old winter ofttimes lingers,
And spring rhododendrons after the snow
   Lift up their beautiful fingers;
But changes may sweep over land and the deep,
Yet nothing disturbs his satisfied sleep.*

In Alma Mater's† halls voices and tears
   May speak the heart's deep yearning,
And oft to the eye Mount Mitchell appears
   When fancy's lights are burning;
But the tolling bell and its mournful knell
Shall bring him no more, for he resteth well.

But a morn shall come, O glorious morn!
   When the trumpet's shrill sounding
Shall reach every soul that ever was born,
   And life anew be bounding;
And God in his might, from the mountain height,
Shall wake his servant to the wondrous sight.

THE CHRIST CHILD.

[Written for the Sunday-school Children of the Mountains.]

'Tis eighteen hundred years gone by,
   While shepherds kept their watch by night,
That one with grandest form drew nigh

---

* Psalm xvii. 15.　　† The University of North Carolina.

To fill their souls with strange delight;
And there on the plain a heavenly strain
Began its glad march o'er the land and the main.

" Tidings of joy," the angel said,
  " I bring to you and all the earth.
You'll find in the manger's lowly bed
  A holy babe of royal birth;
And His 'swaddling's' hem in fair Bethlehem
Shall prove His right to highest diadem."

" Glory to God!" the angels spoke,
  As they praised His name with happy will,
And ne'er hath sweeter music broke
  On earth or the heavenly hill;
And the joyous song of the angel throng
Through the years and the cycles speeds along.

Ten million worlds were in the sky,
  And sacred beauty clothed the scene,
While that sweet song sped soft on high
  'Mid gem, and host, and starry sheen,
And every star in the depths afar
Spoke forth His name whose workmanship they
      are.*

In every land beneath God's sun,
  On the mountain peak and the plain,
Where faith's dear fight is fought and won,
  Men joyful shout the glad refrain,
Till the story old, more bright than gold,
O'er the souls of earth hath its glory rolled.

Yes, so old, when the morning stars
  Shouted their holy matin hymn,
And the rosy light through the stellar bars

*John i.

Glinted creation's wondrous rim,
Thy sweet life began, and the endless span
Of the ages but sweetens Thee to man.

Yet so new, e'en the morning's blush
  On the leaf, on the flower, the stream,
When it wakes the world from the hush
  Of a rapt and enchanting dream,
Is not more new, with its violet hue,
Than the story of Jesus—loving, true.

So, when the holy Xmas morn
  Shall greet our grateful hearts once more,
We'll sing anew, "A child is born "—
  Great Maker of the sea, the shore—
Our banner unfurled, its glory impearled,
Our rapturous song shall gladden the world.

Riverside, N. C., Xmas, 1884.

MARY.

[Lines written in a Lady's Album.]

I NEVER till this moment knew
  The name my gentle friend doth bear;
And then the thought upon me grew,
  Where is another that's more fair?

Historic page and deathless song
  Have crown'd it with immortal hue,
And every age hath borne along
  Its record, beautiful and true.

Old Scotia's sad and fateful queen
  Shall live in every noble soul,
And memory keep her sorrows green
  Where mountains rise and oceans roll.

In our own land, the great and free,
　Another trophy hath it won,
And wreath'd with glory ever be
　The mother of our Washington.

Gentle and sweet, a loved one sat
　At Jesus' feet, while Martha serv'd,
And joyful there she listened at
　The words which Heaven has preserv'd.

But lifted up in matchless grace
　Was she who stood beside the cross,
When Jesus turned his dying face
　And bade dear John to fill his loss.*

I hope my friend will bear in mind
　The name which causes me to write,
And in her earthly journey find
　The peace of God, so sweet and bright.

BEHIND THE VINES.

THERE is a spot upon the river's verge,
　Behind the vines that thickly cluster there,
Where oft my soul doth its petitions urge
　Upon the Master's love and tender care.

The waters, like the stream of human life,
　Are passing, passing, ever passing by,
Sometimes in calm and then in angry strife,
　With breakers white, then gentle as a sigh.

* John xix. 26, 27.

My soul doth catch the river's tender song,
 A farewell song to mountains left behind;
And ever, as its wavelets gush along,
 They leave on peak and glen their blessings kind.

Thus hath my life its many way-marks passed,
 While memory holds them in her fond embrace;
And through the scenes on which her glance is cast
 There gleams a vision of a precious face.

And as my soul sends up its fervent prayer,
 My knees low bent upon the fragrant sod,
Each wingéd thought cuts through the balmy air
 And begs a blessing for it from my God.

O, sweet the faith that comes behind the vines,
 And sweet the face that smiles upon me there;
And sweet the hope which all my heart entwines,
 While for my darling I am locked in prayer!

Riverside, N. C., June, 1885.

LITTLE KATIE.

No toddling step is on the winding stair
 Where once sweet Katie's feet were gliding;
No childish prattle breaks the stillness there,
 Nor sound that answers to my chiding.

No low-toned whisper falls upon my ear
 So soft that love alone may listen;
No tiny hand to wipe away the tear
 Which in my eye doth sadly glisten.

No sound is heard from Katie's sleeping-room,
   That once was fragrant with her breathing;
Nor snow-white arm dispels the thick'ning gloom,
   Around her head its halo wreathing.

No heaving of the gentle little breast,
   The sweetest thing that God has given;
Nor can I see the dear wee face at rest
   As, e'en in dreams, it looked to heaven.

Poor Katie sings not in the earthly nest
   As once she did, her music ringing;
Alone in dreams her songs to me are blest,
   And mem'ry to them still is clinging.

Her step is gone; the warbling voice is still;
   The eye, the form, elude me ever;
And seek her when and where I will,
   The child is gone from earth forever.

The child can never come to me,
   Because she's in the Master's keeping;
But faith's sweet vision lets me see,
   Beyond the dying and the weeping,

That she is by her mother's side,
   Who lately crossed the silent river;
And with dear Robbie for their guide,
   They're resting where the roses quiver.

1886.

LINES WRITTEN IN A YOUNG LADY'S ALBUM.

"WRITE in my book," the maiden said,
   With gentle smile and pleading eye,

And a pleasant nod of her pretty head,
　　Which made me say, " Well, I will try."

What shall I write ?　Did not she say
　　That love had left her " fancy free ?"
And did she not, quite light and gay,
　　Suggest that this would always be?*

If so, her friend will wager now,
　　If Fannie's life shall pass that way,
That some male heart will bleed, I trow,
　　And beg her change to "yea" her "nay."

But I will hope that she may be
　　A happy bride in God's good time,
And in her earthly journey see
　　The peace of heart which is sublime.

LITTLE NICE'S EPITAPH.

[Written for an Afflicted Mother in North Carolina.]

WE will not say our darling's dead,
　　Though gone each charm, so softly pearled;
Though her sweet face and golden head ~
　　May never gladden this bleak world.
There is a land so sweet, so fair,
　　That only faith can glint its shore,
And Nice's feet shall wander there
　　Where Jesus leads forevermore.

---

*She "jumped the broom-stick" in 1886.

LINES

Written on the fly-leaf of a book presented to —— on her twenty-seventh birthday.

WHEN year by year this day shall bring
    Some mem'ries of the past to thee,
With those that to thy bosom cling
    I ask thee to remember me.

TO ——.

[Written on a fly-leaf of a copy of Burns.]

I CANNA tell how true, and sweet, and well
    I hope that all thy life may be;
But trust there'll dwell within thy bosom's cell
    Some kind remembrances of me.

THE LAST ROSE OF SUMMER.

[Moore's " Last Rose of Summer" is exquisite, but it always appeared to the writer to be introduced abruptly. He has therefore ventured to add a stanza for the beginning.]

THERE'S a rose in our garden
    Whose loveliest tint
Is but waiting for autumn
    To give its soft glint;
But my soul fills with sorrow
    As on it I gaze,
For the winds of to-morrow
    Will shorten its days.
"'Tis the last rose of summer," etc.

THE MISSING STEP UPON THE STAIR.

[When the author penned the lines called "The Missing Step upon the Stair" a copy was sent to Col. Silas McDowell, a venerable friend, of Macon County, N. C.—very fond of writing verses himself. In answering the note accompanying the verses, he said, "You were too short; you should have allowed your imagination to have full play." This poem, and the one following, called "The Missing Step upon the Winding Stair," have followed. The dear old friend, however, never saw them, for "God took him."]

AGAIN, when silence in the house was deep,
    Upon my bed my form reclining,
The long, dark shadows o'er my heart did creep,
    Fantastic shapes around me twining.

I listened for a step upon the stair
    That once had thrilled me with its lightness,
And sought once more a form surpassing fair
    To gild my chamber with its brightness.

My hungry soul cried out in bitter pain,
    The darkness 'round me too unbroken,
And eye and ear were constant in their strain
    To catch some sign, of her a token.

And then I knelt with lorn and heaving breast
    To God, who hears the faintest whisper;
Who watches o'er the mountain sparrow's nest,
    And listens to a childish lisper;

And called to Him whose wisdom does not err
    That once again to me be given
The sound of her light step upon my ear,
    Ere heart and soul from earth be riven.

But all was vain; no gentle sound of feet
    Like snow-flakes on the forest falling;
No rustle of the dress my ear did greet,
    Nor voice that answered to my calling.

9

No thrill of joy did cause the soul to bound,
　　As was its wont, to give her greeting;
But mournful silence closed my spirit 'round
　　Unbroken, save my heart's low beating.

And still I'm watching by the winding stair,
　　And wistful through the darkness peering;
But still no form of light and joy is there
　　To give my soul its pleasant greeting.

And now the almond bloom is on my head,
　　And soon I'll reach that solemn ocean
Beyond whose silent waves the happy dead
　　Shall feel no more earth's sad commotion.

And there, on His eternal, peaceful hills,
　　'Mid quiet vales where pleasures quiver,
I'll find her, if the loving Savior wills,
　　And guide her by Life's tree and river.

MULTUM IN PARVO.

Sometimes, while on the road of life,
　　We see a mountain in the distance dim,
Around whose top the fearful strife
　　Of the lightning reddens the cloud's dark rim;
　　　　And we stand in awe
　　　　Of the wondrous law
From whence these things their gorgeous grandeur
　　draw.

Sometimes we stand upon the shore
　　Of gray old ocean, with its rocky bed,

And listen to the breakers' roar
  Beneath the storm king's fierce and awful tread,
      Till the heart stands still
      In the holy thrill
Of a soul that bows to Elohim's will.

Sometimes we measure with our eyes
  The starry worlds upon their endless march,
And turn our eyes o'er the blue skies
  To count each star within the glowing arch ;
      But our numbers fail
      Ere the moonbeams pale
Have faded away o'er the hill and dale.

Sometimes we see an eagle's flight
  Amid the storm and in the angry air,
Careering with a wild delight
  Where thunders roll and forkéd lightnings glare,
      And know that his eye,
      In his flight on high,
Is bright with joy as the clouds roll by.

Sometimes we feel a trembling fear
  When unseen forces in the earth's deep core
Shake all the world from far and near,
      And we scarcely speak,
      For the mountain peak
Has bowed to God, and taught us we are weak.

While thus we gaze upon these things,
  We think that they alone are truly great,
And each one to us ever brings
  Food for the mind, on which we meditate;
      But they'll perish all
      In a moment's call,
From the mighty star to this earthly ball.

But ne'er forget, a drop of dew
　Upon the rose's fresh and tiny leaf
May, by a sun ray clear and true,
　Before it ends its life, so very brief,
　　　　Become a part
　　　　Of the electric dart *
Which tears from the tough oak its mighty heart.

Remember still, a gentle word,
　Though whispered low, as if 'twas but a breath,
Comes like the song of some sweet bird
　To cheer the heart, and to outlive e'en death;
　　　　And o'er and o'er,
　　　　By the radiant shore,
It will thrill and bless us forevermore.
1886.

WEARIN' OF THE GRAY.

AIR: "*Wearin' of the Green.*"

[Written just at the close of the war, and set to music in 1866.
The kind friends who had the music arranged embellished it with
a gray cover.]

OH, Johnny, dear, and did you hear the news that's lately
　　spread,
That never more the Southern Cross must rear its stately
　　head?
The "White and Red's" forbid by law, so Northmen proud-
　　ly say,
Nor you nor I can e'er again be "Wearin' of the Gray."

---

* A drop of dew is filled with electricity.

And when we meet with strangers kind, who take us by the
hand,
Inquiring warmly of the South, our own belovéd land,
We're bound to tell the woeful truth, let cost whate'er it
may,
That some are threatened e'en with death for " Wearin' of
the Gray."

Then since the color we will wear is of the victor's blue,
The children of the " Sunny South" must be to mem'ry
true.
Ah! take the cockade from their hats and tread it 'neath
the feet,
And still, though bruis'd and mangled sad, 'twill speak a
language sweet;
And buried in our heart of hearts the precious words lie
hid,
Where oft they call the bitter tears to wet the drooping
lid;
But let them fall—they do us good through all the mourn-
ful day,
While constant we do call to mind the " Wearin' of the
Gray."

And if at last our fathers' law * be torn from Southland's
heart,
Her sons will take their household gods and far away depart,
Rememb'ring still the whisper'd word to weary wand'rers
giv'n,
That justice pure and perfect rest are found alone in
heav'n.

---

* The Constitution.

Then on some green and distant isle, beneath the setting
  sun,
We'll patient wait the coming time when life and earth
  are done;
Nor even in the dying hour, while passing calm away,
Can we forget or e'er regret the "Wearin' of the Gray."

EXTRACT

From a Speech made on the floor of Congress by the Author, May
4, 1876, on the subject of Fraternity.

"I have no idea of separating the fame of the Gray and
the fame of the Blue. They met in the stern and dreadful
array of battle. They grappled as strong and brave men,
and many of them died with their fingers stiffened around
the flag-staff. God forbid that I should stand up in this
House, or any other part of this broad land, and take away
one iota from their just and glorious fame! This is the
spirit that animates the people of the South, and in this
spirit we are training our children. I will relate a little
circumstance I had from a gentleman who was traveling in
the South—a stranger—in the month of May. He stopped
near a burial-ground, and through the trees could get
glimpses of a number of litt'e girls dressed in white. Each
one had a basket on her arm filled with flowers. On one
side slept the Blue and on the other the Gray, and the
children were singing and strewing flowers upon the graves
of the dead of both armies."

    UNDER the sod and under the clay
    Here sleep the Blue, there sleep the Gray;
    Light be our footsteps as falleth the dew,

Tears for the Gray and tears for the Blue.
Come, sisters, come, let's scatter anew
Wreaths for the Gray and wreaths for the Blue.
Soft be our hearts through all the sweet day,
Smiles for the Blue and smiles for the Gray.

THE DOVE.

" But the dove found no rest for the sole of her foot." (Gen. viii. 9.)

WHEN earth was young and lovely,
   And flowers were fresh and sweet,
God looked on men from heaven,
   His awful judgment-seat,
And He saw that they were guilty
   Of crimes of darkest hue;
Nor stood they in awe of His holy law,
   To which they should be true.

Then God with them was angry,
   And said, in his fierce wrath:
I'll sweep away forever
   These creatures from my path;
Their dwelling-place so beautiful
   Shall perish in a day,
For the waters wild shall be upward piled
   Till all have passed away.

But there was one man faithful,
   Who kindly preached to men,*
And warned them of their sinfulness
   By hill, and dale, and glen;
But never would they listen

---

* 2 Peter ii. 5.

To his prophecies so dark,
But both night and morn they laughed him to
      scorn
As he worked upon the ark.

And when the ark was finished,
   Well pitched without, within,
The animals of the kingdom
   Began to enter in;
And Noah and his family,
   Truth-loving persons, eight,
With strong faith in God and his mighty rod,
   Passed in and closed the gate.

Then came the rain in fury,
   And gave the flood its birth,
Till the fierce and maddened billows
   Swept o'er the startled earth,
And its dazed inhabitants,
   With terror and despair,
Fled in sore affright to the mountain height
   To only perish there.

For upward foamed the waters
   Till all the earth was gone,
Save the tallest of the uplands,
   Which o'er the breakers shone;
And 'mid the awful ruin
   Of man, and beast, and bird,
A woman's wild shriek on the highest peak
   Was the saddest sound earth heard.

But God, from out his glory,
   Looked on men's daughters fair,
Whom the sons of God had taken,*

---

* Genesis vi. 2.

Their destiny to share;
And when he saw them weeping,
  Their hearts with anguish riven,
He caught their tears on the sunbeam's spears
  And formed His bow in heaven.

And when the billows' raging
  Had hid the world from sight,
And the thunder of the tempest
  Was booming in its might,
The ark was grandly sailing
  Above the foam and spray,
And God's servant's song was borne along
  Upon the fearful way.

For when the highest mountains
  Came into view again,
And the deep had stopped her fountains
  From ocean unto main,
The dove was sent for tidings
  Of the world beneath the flood;
But the gentle thing, with its tireless wing,
  Found neither rest nor food.

But with her rapid pinions
  She sought the ark once more,
Till the waters were abated
  To the ocean's wonted shore;
For while the billows mounted
  O'er all the earth below,
No place would suit for the sole of her foot,
  So to the ark she flew.

So, to our Father's glory,
  When 'round our feeble bark
The waves of sin are dashing,

There's safety in God's ark.*
And it is grand in finish,
  With room for all to come ;
And the ship will sail on the upward gale
  Till we are safe at home.

TRUE BEAUTY.

[Written for a Child's Album.]

There's beauty in the gentle form,
  The rosy cheek, the laughing eye,
The beaming face with pleasure warm,
  And in the forehead fair and high.

There's beauty still of nobler kind,
  Because it never here will fade;
It is the beauty of the mind,
  Which lives when all beside's decayed.

But better yet than these, than all,
  Is the sweet beauty of the soul,
Which still shall live when angels tall
  God's circling years shall onward roll.

THE MISSING STEP UPON THE WINDING STAIR.

[This little poem can no longer be considered an imaginary feeling of the writer, as it comes to him now with all the anguish of reality.]

The stricken days to me are passing on,
  But silence still is on the winding stair;
Nor can I catch a sound of her that's gone,
  Though heart and ear are ever listening there.

---

* The Church is a safe refuge for God's children.

When morn has come, and all its glories beam
   Across the hills and o'er the mountain peak,
I fondly dream—'tis only but a dream—
   That she will come, her old sweet words to speak.

When noon shall throw its threads of burnished gold
   On walks and paths traversed so long ago,
The sweetest thrill my spirit there shall hold
   Is that her love at last will soothe my woe.

When eventide, with soft and mellow light,
   Shall gild the clouds and glint the deep blue sky,
My heart will throb, amid its bitter blight,
   That she will come and bless me ere I die.

When midnight glows with many million stars,
   And worlds are shining in their far-off home,
My soul will leap beyond its earthly bars,
   And beg of God that she to me may come.

And e'en in sleep my soul will linger still,
   And anxious wait, with more than miser care,
For God to send her by his holy will
   To meet me yet upon the winding stair.

But O, I know that this can never be,
   For, lifted up in fearful wrath and foam,
The waves of death rolled o'er life's troubled sea,
   And parted us for all earth's years to come !

And then I ask, when through the clouds I see
   A world of joy not made by human hand,
If she will know me in eternity,
   And love and bless me in the better land.

I wonder if that world of light and love
    Contains for higher flights a winding stair,
Upon whose steps her graceful form will move
    To bid me welcome in the upper air.

I only know I'm on the winding stair,
    And wistful waiting for her slender feet
To fall once more, like dew-drops on the air,
    And give my soul a comfort rich and sweet.

But knowing they can never come again,
    As once they did, when to my soul they spoke,
In heaven, I trust, there'll be no parting pain,
    And ne'er a loving, faithful heart be broke.

Washington City, D. C., January 8, 1887.

LINES

Written in the Album of Mrs. H., of Maine.

OUR homes in life in distant States have been;
    Yours in the East, where the Atlantic's thunder
Breaks on the coast; mine, where with silver sheen
    The Southern Cross beams on savannas under.

From out your home the gallant men in Blue
    Came forth at once to meet our sons in battle,
And every spot where they their claymores drew
    Shall tell of those who faced the volley's rattle.

Together on many a dreadful field
    These brothers true have left to us this story:
Their beating hearts were their loved country's shield,
    And side by side the dead ones sleep in glory.

The shrill reveille in the early morn,
  The sweet tattoo when evening stars are shining,*
The wild bird's song among the rustling corn,
  Break not the rest in which they are reclining.

Ten thousand cannon on the flaming ridge,
  With rifles bright in more than countless number,
May wrap in fire the valley, peak, and bridge,
  But nothing earthly can disturb their slumber.

The rushing steed, the banners in the air,
  The victors' shout, the wounded and the dying,
And breaking hearts for those who are not there,
  They heed no more where peaceful they are lying.

I love to think that both the Blue and Gray
  Have common fame which naught on earth can sever;
And though hate may seek to tear it all away,
  Yet, thanks to God! their fame is one forever!

Why should the living not be friends as well
  As those who side by side in death are sleeping,
Since interests more than my poor pen can tell
  Are in our hands for safest, dearest keeping?
Closing hours of Forty-eighth Congress, 1885.

---

*No soldier will ever forget the sweetness of the tattoo after a
day of toil and danger.

WAR AND ITS BURDENS.—ARMIES OF THE WORLD.

Countries.	Regular Army.	Annual Cost of Army.
Austro-Hungary............	284,071	$ 49,116,248
Argentine Republic........	7,518	5,800,000
Belgium..................	47,084	9,208,046
Bolivia..................	3,021	2,148,000
Brazil...................	13,500	7,466,120
Canada...................	2,000	3,840,000
Chili...................	13,926	16,326,095
China...................	300,000	75,000,000
Colombia	4,000	....
Cuba....................	25,653	....
Denmark	35,727	2,461,955
Egypt...................	10,900	....
France	529,269	121,061,600
Germany.................	445,402	84,968,140
Great Britain............	181,971	90,901,630
Greece	29,368	3,312,140
Guatemala	2,180	....
Hawaii..................	400	....
India, British	190,476	87,201,250
Italy...................	750,765	41,098,611
Japan...................	37,790	9,263,713
Luxembourg	377	75,680
Mexico..................	22,330	8,252,352
Netherlands..............	65,113	8,464,000
Nicaragua	703	....
Norway..................	18,750	1,628,440
Persia..................	30,000	3,800,000
Peru	13,200	....
Portugal	33,994	5,099,105
Roumania................	19,512	5,463,550
Russia	780,081	125,508,474
Servia	18,000	2,072,890
Spain...................	152,895	24,524,415
Sweden	40,758	4,322,860
Switzerland	117,500	3,341,260
Turkey.. ....*.....	160,417	23,841,064
United States............	26,383	39,429,603
Uruguay.................	4,500	....
Venezuela	3,000	....

—Spofford's American Almanac.

Notwithstanding the magnitude of the regular armies of the world, as shown on the preceding page, Von Moltke and Bismarck both clamored in the German Reichstag for an increase of the German Army, which is now 445,402 strong, at an annual cost of $85,-000,000. The effect of this, if carried out, will be an increase of all the European, and perhaps the Asiatic, armies.

Let us have peace.—*Gen. Grant.*

"And He shall judge among the nations, and shall rebuke many people; and they shall beat their swords into plowshares, and their spears into pruning-hooks; nation shall not lift up sword against nation, neither shall they learn war any more." (Isa. ii. 4.)

'TIS nineteen hundred years since when
The Lord of Life came unto men,
Himself the gentle Prince of Peace,
Who taught the world that war should cease;
Who never spake an unjust word,
Or bade a mortal draw a sword;
Who ne'er oppressed a man or child
In city full or desert wild;
Who never caused a tear to flow
From human kind because of woe;
Who never had His guard of state
Upon His royal will to wait;
Who ne'er had armies at His will
With sword and lance to thrust and kill;
Who ne'er with royal purple robe
Sat out as if to rule the globe;
But who, with love and matchless grace,
Was brother of the human race.

And yet—great God, inspire my pen!—
He was the very prince of men;
For when He came to visit earth,
And bless the world by His glad birth,

Though cradled in the ox's stall,
Where it was feeding by the wall,
Or resting on his mother's knee
With not a sign of majesty—
Except what was to men unknown—
The swaddling clothes should hint a throne
Above thy stable, Bethlehem,
Brighter than monarch's fairest gem,
The wondrous star stood still at last,
And o'er the scene its glory cast;
While coming from the glowing plain,
Where angels sang their sweet refrain,
The Magi, kneeling at His feet,
Expressed their joy in praises meet,
Which every loving soul doth stir,
And gave their gifts of gold and myrrh.

Yes, what a wondrous prince was He,
One with God in eternity,
Before the morning stars e'er shone
In all their glory 'round His throne;
Before a single world was thrown
By power which truly was His own,*
To take its place in the grand race
Amid the fields of endless space;
Or e'en before the Spirit's might
Had spoke the words, " Let there be light;"
And who was Chief when there were sent,
Along the glowing firmament,
Ten million worlds, with banners fair,
To flash and sparkle in the air,
And shout with energy divine,
" The glory; Lord, 's forever thine!"

* John i. 3.

If Jesus had designed to reign
As monarch, with a monarch's train,
Behold the worlds he brought to view
Along the sky's cerulean blue,
Where, numbered with our earthly ball,
He was the maker of them all;
And, ready at a moment's word,
Twelve legion angels would have stirred*
In arms of heavenly temper keen,
With eyes of fire, and lofty mien;
With wings of light, and pennons fair,
Their armor flashing in the air,
Above, below, upon the hill,
Waiting to see their Prince's will;
But, wondrous thought! He was so great,
So skilled to plan, and to create,
That with amazing power and grace
He spun the worlds in far-off space;
Caused all the wheels of worlds to go,
The suns to shine, the stars to glow;
And, painting all with fingers deft,
He placed the mountains by his heft;
Set oceans on their endless roll,
And poised the worlds from pole to pole;
When finished all, He paused to rest,
That He might build a sparrow's nest.

Behold the petty kings of earth
Who strut in purple from their birth,
And teach in story and in song
"The king can never do a wrong;"
Forgetting God, the one true King,

---

* Matthew xxvi. 53.

They on the world such anguish bring—
A grief so deep, a woe so fell—
That human pen it may not tell;
And burdens 'round the cabin door,
Forever pressing down the poor,
Until the soul grows faint and sad
O'er miseries by earth's children had.

Great God! when, rising to our view,
Earth's battle-fields pass in review,
And, tracing down the track of time,
We see them in their shock sublime—
The Roman tall, the graceful Greek,
Who, dead, yet by their deeds they speak;
The Briton, and the child of France,
Who by the javelin and lance,
On many a famed and martial field,
Were thrown beneath each bloody shield;
The stalwart Scot, the Irish brave,
Who died their liberty to save;
And all the brave in the Old World,
Where war's dread banner was unfurled;
And coming westward to the New,
Where met in strife the Gray and Blue;
And, calling up the widows' tears,
Their anguished hearts, their frenzied fears;
The orphan's cry and lonely head,
Each dear protector with the dead;
The shallow graves which held our own,
Their bloody blankets 'round them thrown;
And all the agony and pain,
Though wrapped in glory be the slain,
Which round the field of battle glows
Where sleep together the brave foes,

We beg of Thee to show Thy might,
And stop forever the mad fight.

THE GOVERNOR'S LAST PARDON.

Dying Alexander Stephens said: "You think that because I have been ill so many times and got well, I shall get well now, but you are mistaken; I will not recover. Where is that letter by that woman in the penitentiary? I think she has suffered enough. As near as I can tell, she has no friends. Bring me that paper, that I may sign her pardon." A gentleman standing by, thinking this too great a responsibility for the sick man, said, "Governor, you are very sick now; perhaps you had better wait till to-morrow; you may feel stronger, and you may feel better." Then the eye of the old Governor flashed, and he said, "I know what I am about." Putting his signature to that pardon, he wrote the last word he ever wrote, for then the pen fell from his pale, and rheumatic, and dying hand forever. O my soul, how beautiful that the closing hours of life should be spent in helping one who had no helper!—*Georgia Newspaper.*

THE good old man was drawing near
The river, flushed with human fear.

His feet were in the waters cold,
And near him then the billows rolled.

The feeble form, the brilliant eye *
Said plainly 'twas his time to die.

Nor did he fear the heaving tide,
But calmly viewed the other side,

Where bands, to human eye unseen,
Were waiting in their splendid sheen,

---

* It is often true that the eye of a good person grows very bright as death approaches.

To lift him from the waters cold,
And give him welcome to the fold.

And while his feet were passing o'er
There came unto him from the shore—

The other shore, the happy shore
Which he had never seen before—

Seraphic music from the throng
Who beautified the shore along.

"Come, father, come," they joyful sang,
And O how sweet the music rang,

As, lifted o'er the ranks around
Which covered all fair Salem's ground,

They waved his palm, his robe of white,
Which glittered in the holy light,

And bade him come, they could not wait,
But wished to see him pass the gate.*

But suddenly the old man stayed
His parting feet, and gently said

To those who watched beside his bed,
With rev'rence for his honor'd head,

"You think that I'll be well again,
And health and wonted spirits gain;

"But you are wrong, I'll never be
Upon this earth from suffering free;

---

* Revelation xxi. 25.

"And voices now are calling me
To pass life's utmost boundary;

"And you may think I'm wrong in mind,
But wait a moment, you shall find.

"That I have time, while near the end,
To act for one who has no friend:

"Bring the petition sent to me
By the woman who would be free."

And there, while nearing the last shore,
He ope'd for her the prison door;

When lo! from on the other shore
The throng in white sent greetings o'er;

And far away, o'er hills of heaven,
A shout of joy for him was given.

Then, calm and mild, death's stream he trod,
To dwell forever with his God.

Dear Savior, when my time has come
To pass the river's chilling foam,

May heart and soul be gentle too,
To life's best feelings still be true;

So, when I reach the farther side,
I'll find among the glorified

A welcome warm, a sweet embrace
From those who passed me in life's race.

THE CAMP-MEETING.

[Dedicated to the Memory of the Sainted Dead.]

HIGH up along the slopings of the Carolina mountains,
Where westward turn so rapidly the waters of the rivers;
Where Tahkeeostee rushes toward the foaming Holston,
And all the streams are seeking the mighty Mississippi;

And when they all have gathered into its raging currents,
And mingled with the spoutings from off the Rocky
    Mountains;
From out the forest masses and worlds of prairie flowers;
And, shrieking, foaming, dashing, go thundering to the
    ocean;

Adown the French Broad valley, below the Swannanoa,
Upon the hills of Buncombe, the old and famous county,
Where a college now is standing in pretty Weaverville,
Along the famed old highway that leads to County Yancey;

I call to mind a vision, a sweet and joyful memory,
Of times that now are olden, and happiness all golden,
In the sunny days of childhood, when, with our darling
    mother,
We camped at the camp-meeting, to hear the holy gospel.

The stand was large and spacious for the holding of the
    people,
The altar fixed with neatness to welcome there the mourn-
    ers;
And when we reached the meeting, the neighbors all were
    gathering,
And every tent was filling by bosoms that were willing

To labor for the Savior, in singing and in praying,
And to show to all His glory by telling the old story,

And pointing out with gladness the peaceful road to heaven,
That nothing might be lacking at holy, solemn Salem.*

It was in the sweet October, when all the woods were saffron,
Deep green and palish yellow, with touches of carnation,
Which make our gorgeous forests so wonderful and lovely,
From the frost-work of the hickory to the variegated maple.†

And on the mountains distant, above the Reems Creek valley,
Around the lofty Pinnacle, and stern old giant Craggy,
The clouds were piled like billows upon the restless ocean,
And the sun's departing splendors were on them softly shining.

The apple-trees were bending beneath their juicy loading,
And all the earth was giving good token of the harvest,
And teaching us the lesson that while the earth is standing
There nevermore shall fail us the sowing and the reaping.

How faithful is our Father! the Lord of earth and heaven,
Whose hands are always open to bless His loving children;
Whose bosom is a refuge from toil, and pain, and sorrow,
For servants who are faithful in all things great and little.

Thus to the sacred camping our happy way we'd wended
Along the racing river and up the river mountains,
Till we were snugly settled beneath the tent's low roofing,
And eventide was resting on the hills and on the meeting.

---

* The name of the camp-ground.
† The forests of Western North Carolina are exquisitely beautiful in October.

Then, as the hour of twilight was hiding the lone forest,
And the starry hosts of heaven were glowing in the ether,
The preacher's trumpet sounding called all the worship-
ers
To come unto the altar to make the sweet beginning.

Sweet was the prayer of gratitude which to the Lord as-
cended
From strong and holy brothers, and tender, loving sisters,
That once more in life's glad journey they'd joined their
hearts in giving
Sweet praises to the Master, their keeper and their maker.

How wondrous was the lighting of the hallowed place of
meeting,
As on a wooden platform, with soil alone for covering,
The flaming of the torches upon the stand and altar
Reflected back the faces of the worshipers of Jesus.

Tall and strong was the good preacher, who went into the
pulpit
And gazed upon the brothers, and on the faithful sisters,
With eyes of deep affection and tenderest emotion,
To preach the opening sermon on that occasion holy.

Long years had he been telling the story of the passion
Of Jesus, our Redeemer, who came unto the sinful,
And walked amid earth's sorrows, the humble, poor, and
lowly,
To show the road to heaven, Himself the door to enter.

Uncle Jacob* was the preacher, whose text and earnest
calling
Resounded in our hearing upon that sweet occasion:

---

* Rev. Jacob Weaver.

"Ho! every one that thirsteth, come ye unto the waters,
And satisfy your thirsting in the sweet gospel fountain."

His hymn was in accordance with the text's most precious
teaching,
For it taught the soothing doctrine that the pearly gates
of Eden *
Stand open eve and morning to let believers enter,
For night shall never darken the city sweet and restful.

And when the sermon ended, in which were kindly blended
The most earnest admonition with words of tender comfort,
The congregation kneeling, with sweetest, truest feeling
Drew near the throne of mercy, led by our cousin Montra-
ville.†

And there, at dear old Salem, God sent his Spirit holy
The souls of men to quicken, His own word to glorify;
And many came to Jesus whose after-lives were given
To His dear and joyous service forever and forever.

But soon the hour was nearing when the happy, peaceful
meeting
Should end its holy service, and all the friends be parting;
When, standing in the pulpit to give a parting blessing,
A form in black apparel,‡ in whose hands the gospel
weapon

Had oft been truly shining, as the sacred hours were going,
Spoke there unto the people, and thanked them for their
kindness,
Their patience truly gentle to neighbors and to strangers,

---

* Rev. xxi. 25. † Rev. M. M. Weaver. ‡ Rev. E. F. Sevier, P. E.

Which things were duly written in the good book of
    Heaven.

" But there is one lone stranger, whose feet are white with
    travel,
Whose locks are wet with dewdrops as he was gently
    standing
Beside the altar railing, or near the spacious arbor,
Whose pure, benign demeanor should have given him
    warmest greeting;

" Whom some have not invited, nor gave to him a welcome,
Though lovely in his person and in his manner gracious;
Who truly could have bless'd them, and gave them double
    portion
For all they'd to him given, on the earth, or in sweet
    heaven."

Just near the gracious preacher a little boy was standing,
Who listened in grave wonder to the preacher's painful
    story;
Who gazed upon the people to see the gentle stranger,
To take him to his bosom and satisfy his hunger.

But the people all were weeping, and looking at the
    preacher,
As his voice of touching sadness fell full upon their hear-
    ing;
And none of them did answer the little boy so eager,
So he went unto his mother and asked her in a whisper

Who was the slighted stranger who had no place for rest-
    ing,
That he might bring him thither to sup with him and
    mother.
The tear-drops then did glitter beneath the lady's lashes

As she took him to her bosom and softly said, "Thy Savior."

Then said the little fellow, " I'll be His friend forever,
If He will with us tarry in our home beside the river;
Nor shall His feet be smitten by the chilling winds of winter;
Nor night his locks bedewing, for we'll have Him in our keeping."

Not many now are living who were at the happy meeting
Upon the hill of Salem, in French Broad's goodly valley;
For they've crossed the river over, and on the hills of heaven
They've had a happier meeting, which never will be ended.

But in the raging battle, and in the lonely prison;
Down in the lowly valley, and in the mighty city,
The boy has loved the stranger who 'round the camp did wander
At the long-ago camp-meeting at holy, solemn Salem.

THE MOUNTAIN CROSS.

[Just after the traveler passes the celebrated Painted Rock, at the border of North Carolina and Tennessee, he will find the train passing between two stupendous mountains, the French Broad River between the two. Standing on the rear platform, he will see, near the top of the mountain, a white cross, which seems a way-mark for heaven.]

As down the dashing river
    The trav'ler speeds his way,
He sees upon the mountain

Above him far away,
Just where the rock is riven
By the bursting of a flood,*
On that awful height, a cross, snow-white,
To point his soul to God.

Down there the boiling waters
Arise, and foam, and swell,
And in a voice of thunder
They startle all the dell;
But high above the rushing,
Just near the peaceful sky,
That most holy sign of a love divine
Swells out to greet the eye.

And while the eye is gazing
Upon that sign so sweet,
He forgets the rushing river
Where the mad waters meet;
And his soul is filled with gladness
That in his mountain land,
With a matchless grace, for the human race,
The Lord holds out His hand.

I love thee, racing river,
I love each lofty crag;
I love the mighty mountains,
The home of the fleet stag;
But dearer to my vision,
And sweeter to my heart,
Is the land of the leal, so dear, so real,
Where loved ones never part.

---

*It is the opinion of scientists that a great lake once covered
the valley of the French Broad.

Roll on, thou rushing river!
  Stand up, ye mountains tall!
And rock, and hill, and cañon
  Grace well this earthly ball;
And white cross on the mountain,
  Stand out on the high peak,
And with thy true hand point to the sweet land
  Which trav'lers all should seek!

THE END.

www.ingramcontent.com/pod-product-compliance
Lightning Source LLC
Chambersburg PA
CBHW030903050726
47500CB00009B/1005